Acting Edition

Rodgers & Hammerstein's
Me and Juliet

Music by
Richard Rodgers

Book & Lyrics by
Oscar Hammerstein II

Edited by Harold Glick

FOR PRODUCTION INQUIRIES

UNITED STATES AND CANADA
info@concordtheatricals.com
1-866-979-0447

UNITED KINGDOM AND EUROPE
licensing@concordtheatricals.co.uk
020-7054-7298

Each title is subject to availability from Concord Theatricals Corp., depending upon country of performance. Please be aware that *ME AND JULIET* may not be licensed by Concord Theatricals Corp. in your territory. Professional and amateur producers should contact the nearest Concord Theatricals Corp. office or licensing partner to verify availability.

CHARACTERS

JEANIE – Chorus Singer
BOB – Electrician
LARRY – Assistant Stage Manager
SIDNEY – Electrician
MAC – Stage Manager
DARIO – Conductor
HERBIE – Candy Counter Boy
RUBY – Company Manager
CHARLIE (ME) – Featured Lead
LILY (JULIET) – Singing Principal
JIM (DON JUAN) – Principal Dancer
SUSIE (CARMEN) – Principal Dancer
GEORGE – Second Assistant Stage Manager
BETTY – Successor to Susie as Principal Dancer
CHRIS – Rehearsal Pianist
MILTON – Drummer
STU – Bass Fiddle Player
BUZZ – Principal Dancer
VOICE OF MR. HARRISON – Producer
VOICE OF MISS DAVENPORT – Choreographer
HILDA – An Aspirant for a dancing part
MARCIA – Another Aspirant for a dancing part
SADIE – An Usher
MILDRED – Another Usher
ENSEMBLE – Company, Stage Crew, Audience, Theatre Patrons

MUSICAL NUMBERS

ACT I

00. ["OVERTURE"]
01. ["OPENING"]
02. ["A VERY SPECIAL DAY"] . . . . Jeanie
03. ["THAT'S THE WAY IT HAPPENS"] . . . . Jeanie
04. ["THAT'S THE WAY IT HAPPENS" (REPRISE)] . . . . Larry
05. [OVERTURE TO "ME AND JULIET" (DARIO'S OVERTURE)] . . Dario
. . . . and Orchestra
06. [OPENING OF "ME AND JULIET)" (PROLOGUE)"] . . . . . Lily (Juliet),
. . . . Charlie (Me) and Girls
07. ["MARRIAGE TYPE LOVE"] . . . . . Lily (Juliet), Charlie (Me) and Girls
08. ["MARRIAGE TYPE LOVE" (ENCORE)] . . . .Bob
09. ["CHANGE OF SCENE"]
10. ["SCENE ON LIGHT BRIDGE"] . . . . Bob
11. ["KEEP IT GAY"] . . . .Bob
12. ["KEEP IT GAY" (DANCE)] . . . . Chorus
13. ["SCENE 5"] . . . .Chorus
14. ["THE AUDITION (KEEP IT GAY- REPRISE)"] . . . . Betty
15. ["THE AUDITION CONTINUES"] . . . . Jeanie
16. ["THE BIG BLACK GIANT"] . . . . Larry
17. ["NO OTHER LOVE"] . . . . Jeanie and Larry
18. ["INCIDENTAL ON DARK STAGE"]
19.["DANCE IN THE ALLEY"]
20. ["THE BIG BLACK GIANT" (REPRISE)] . . . . Ruby
21. ["IT'S ME"] . . . . Betty (Carmen) and Jeanie
22. ["IT'S ME" (INCIDENTAL)]
23. ["DRESSING ROOM"] . . . . Jeanie
24. ["IT'S ME (CHANGE OF SCENE)"]
25. ["INCIDENTAL ON LIGHT BRIDGE"]
26. ["FINALE ACT 1"] . . . . Lily (Juliet)

ACT II

27. ["ENTR'ACTE"]
27A ["ACT II OPENING CURTAIN"]
28. ["INTERMISSION TALK"] . . . . Herbie, Company

[MUSIC 00 – "OVERTURE"]

ACT I

Scene One

[MUSIC 01 – "OPENING"]

(The curtain rises on a bare stage. The proscenium of the "ME AND JULIET" show is off centre to the left so that we see the off stage area on the right. In the foreground the light bridge is seen lowered halfway to the floor. A rehearsal piano is set stage left and backstage there are property boxes. The Stage Manager's desk is seen at stage right.)

*(**JEANIE** is seen sitting at the piano playing. **GEORGE** enters right and is met by **TWO BOYS** who enter from left.)*

GEORGE. Half hour! – Half hour!

*(**SIDNEY**, the electrician, comes on from up right. **GEORGE** enters at the same time from left.)*

BOYS. Hi George!

SIDNEY. *(Enter cross centre.)* How about some lights!

GEORGE. Hey Louis! Give us some lights.

VOICE FROM OFFSTAGE. OK.

(The lights come on.)

GEORGE. *(Calling.)* Half hour! Half hour!

   (**SIDNEY** *goes to ladder with lamp and starts to work.* **JEANIE** *rises from piano striking dissonant chords with a bang.* **MILTON** *the drummer has entered up right and starts to set his drums above the piano.)*

MILTON. *(Entering.) (Looking at* **JEANIE**.*)* That sounds kinda modern.

   (He goes off left.)

   (**TWO CHORUS GIRLS** *enter on up left cross right.)*

JEANIE. *(Cross left of ladder.) (To* **SIDNEY**.*)* I've been stood up. Bob told me he was coming in early.

SIDNEY. He told me he was coming early too. He's supposed to be here right now helping me.

   (**SIDNEY** *crosses right to below portal.)*

   (**JEANIE** *walks over to right of* **SIDNEY**.*)*

Jeanie, how long have you been going with Bob?

JEANIE. Since the show opened – about six months.

SIDNEY. This the first time he stood you up?

JEANIE. No.

SIDNEY. Don't you ever get sore at him?

JEANIE. Sure I do.

   (Smiling, cross center.)

But he's always so sorry when he does anything wrong. He's like a kid.

SIDNEY. *(Sarcastically.)* Yeah. He's cute.

JEANIE. *(Leaning on ladder.)* You don't like Bob, do you?

SIDNEY. I like him alright. I'm up on this bridge with him all the time. We have a lot of laughs together. If that's all you want out of him he's fine. But if anybody gets an idea she can make him into something better than he is, she's letting herself in for something, that's all I gotta say. Excuse me for butting in.

JEANIE. Oh, don't apologize, I get a lot of advice about Bob from everybody.

> *(**JEANIE** crosses over to the Stage Manager's desk.)*

> *(**HERBIE, CHRIS, MILTON** and **STU** enter from left.)*

HERBIE. Come on kids it'll be curtain time before you know it. Come on let's go, let's go.

> *(**CHRIS, MILTON** and **STU** starts to play.)*

Know what we're doing, Sidney. We're getting up a Trio.

> *(A girl and boy enter left and cross the stage together. They are followed by another girl who crosses in a hurry. **HERBIE** turns to **CHRIS, MILTON** and **STU**.)*

That's it kids.

> *(To **SIDNEY**.)*

We're going on Arthur Godfrey's Talent Scouts.

SIDNEY. You going to be the Scout?

HERBIE. Sure. Can you see me sitting up there at the desk next to Arthur Godfrey?

SIDNEY. Yeh. I can hear you too. He'll ask you where you come from and you'll say Brooklyn and everybody'll clap.

>   (**GEORGE** *enters from up right and meets two* **GIRLS** *and a boy who enter left.*)

GIRL. *(To* **GEORGE.***)* Hi ya George – going to give us a little music on your whistle?

GEORGE. Better get made up first.

GIRL. We'll put on our smocks.

2ND GIRL. On the way down to get our costumes –

[MUSIC 02 – "A VERY SPECIAL DAY"]

GEORGE. OK.

>   *(They exit left and right.)*

JEANIE. *(Sitting at desk.)* Oh dear!
AM I BUILDING SOMETHING UP
THAT REALLY ISN'T THERE?
DO I MAKE A BIG ROMANCE
OF A SMALL AFFAIR?
SHOULD I BE MORE PRACTICAL,
AS FRIENDS WOULD HAVE ME BE?
… BEING PRACTICAL IS VERY HARD FOR ME.
I WAKE UP EACH MORNING *(Rise.)*
WITH A FEELING IN MY HEART
THAT TO-DAY WILL BE A VERY SPECIAL DAY.
(Crossing left to center stage.) I KEEP RIGHT ON CLINGING
TO THAT FEELING IN MY HEART
'TIL THE WINDS OF EV'NING BLOW MY DREAMS AWAY.
LATER ON, AT BEDTIME,
WHEN MY WORLD HAS COME APART
AND I'M IN MY FAR FROM FANCY NEGLIGEE
WITH A PIECE OF TOAST TO MUNCH
AND A NICE HOT CUP OF TEA,

I BEGIN TO HAVE A HUNCH
THAT TOMORROW'S GOING TO BE
A VERY SPECIAL DAY FOR ME.

LORRAINE'S VOICE. Jeanie, would you get sore if I offered some advice?

OTHER VOICES. You can do better than him, Jeanie.

Why an electrician?

> (**JEANIE** *cross right to desk.*)

How'd you happen to tie up with a guy like that?

How does a thing like that start?

JEANIE. How does it start?

[MUSIC 03 – "THAT'S THE WAY IT HAPPENS"]

> (*The music changes now and* **JEANIE** *sings against it as if in answer to all the questions she is used to hearing.*)

YOU'RE A GIRL FROM CHICAGO
ON THE ROAD WITH A SHOW,
NOT A SOUL IN NEW HAVEN
YOU CAN SAY YOU KNOW.
YOU WISH YOU WERE A MILE OR
SO FROM MICHIGAN LAKE,
HOME WITH YOUR MOTHER AND A T-BONE STEAK.
THEN ALONG COMES A FELLOW
WITH A SMILE LIKE A KID,
AND HE GETS YOUR ATTENTION
WITH A TIMELY BID.
HE SAYS HE KNOWS A BISTRO
WHERE THEY GIVE YOU A BREAK
WITH FRENCH FRIED POTATOES AND A T-BONE STEAK!

> (*She crosses quickly to ladder.*)

YOU ARE SHY AND UNCERTAIN,

BUT HE PLEADS AND YOU YIELD,
AND YOU DON'T HAVE AN INKLING
THAT YOU'RE SIGNED AND SEALED.
BY MERELY TELLING SOMEONE
YOU'D BE GLAD TO PARTAKE
OF FRENCH FRIED POTATOES AND A T-BONE STEAK.
THAT'S THE WAY IT HAPPENS,
THAT'S THE WAY IT HAPPENS.
THAT'S THE WAY IT HAPPENED TO ME!

(She crosses right and exits.)

GIRL. Girls maybe we should ask for a raise.

BOY. *(At piano.)* Hey, did you see this in Variety?

(Reading.)

"Musical pays off. Backers of 'Me and Juliet' out of red and due to collect plenty on unconventional dance opera".

(Follow this by entrance of **BOB.***)*

BOB. *(Move right of ladder.)* Hello Sidney.

SIDNEY. Well!

BOB. *(Works on cable.)* Am I late?

SIDNEY. Yes, you're late.

BOB. I just ran into a guy I knew.

SIDNEY. That was nice.

BOB. You're not sore, are you, angel face?

(He messes **SIDNEY***'s hair up.)*

SIDNEY. Get to work on that cable. We haven't got much time.

> (**BOB** *starts to work on a cable coiled on the
> floor by the step ladder. More of the* **COMPANY**
> *enter, starts to cross stage, are met by a* **GIRL**
> *in a short smock upstage and stop and talk,
> perhaps show writings to her.)*

Jeanie was here just now.

BOB. Why didn't she wait for me?

> (**SIDNEY** *gives him a sarcastic look.)*

Was she sore?

> (**SIDNEY** *shrugs his shoulders.)*

Guess I'll have to talk my way out of it, huh?

> (*He chuckles.)*

She's a sweet kid.

SIDNEY. (*Looking hard at him.)* Ever think you'd like to
marry Jeanie?

> (**SID** *sits on ladder.)*

BOB. Me? Not oh your life! ...I know <u>too many</u> guys who
got hooked. You know what happens soon's you get
married? Right away the dame's got to go to the dentist
and get all her teeth fixed. You get a bill for three
hundred bucks. That's only the beginning...

SIDNEY. (*Getting angry on* **JEANIE***'s behalf.)* Ah, she
wouldn't have you anyway. I'm surprised she even talks
to you.

> (*A puzzled expression crosses* **BOB***'s face. He's
> not quite sure whether* **SIDNEY** *is kidding or
> not.)*

One of the best lookin' babes in the show. You'd think
she could get something better'n a baboon like you.

(**BOB** *has grabbed* **SIDNEY** *by the collar of his shirt, and by the seat of his trousers, and lifts him up so that he's nearly clear off the ground.* **CHRIS**, **MILTON** *and* **STU** *stop playing and watch.*)

Hey what are you doing? Cut it out, Bob! I got the lamp in my hand! Want me to break it? I was only kiddin'.

(**BOB** *takes* **SIDNEY** *right center.*)

Cut it out, I tell you! You damn fool!

BOB. Who's a damn fool?

(**BOB**, *still holding* **SIDNEY**'s *trousers with one hand, garrotes him with the other arm.*)

SIDNEY. (*His voice muffled, choking.*) You're hurting me!

(**BOB** *releases him.*)

What the hell's the matter with you, anyway?

(**BOB** *walks away, roaring with laughter. More of the* **COMPANY** *enter, sense something wrong. Others whisper to them to report what has happened – all remain upstage.*)

(**SIDNEY** *feels the humiliation and frustration of a small man bullied by a big one.*)

You're a cute kid! Funny as hell!

(**BOB** *laughs even louder.*)

What's the matter with you? You're getting like you used to be!

(**BOB** *stops laughing suddenly.*)

BOB. What's that?

(*JEANIE enters right dressed in the knee-length smock the girls wear before they go downstairs to put on their costumes. She remains upstage, unseen by the others.*)

SIDNEY. (*Staring back at* BOB *with the reckless courage of panic.*) I said –

BOB. I heard what you said.

(*He walks slowly over to* SIDNEY *and stands in front of him.*)

And don't ever say that again.

(*Raising his voice to a shout.*)

You hear?

(*Lowering his voice again.*)

Don't you ever... I'm not like I used to be – and it's damn lucky for you I'm not.

(*He stands scowling down at* SIDNEY *as if not quite sure whether he will throttle him or not. Then he becomes conscious of* JEANIE's *presence. Embarrassed, he switches to his other self – the big charm boy.*)

Hello, Jeanie...

(*A nervous laugh.*)

What do you know about this guy Sidney? Trying to kid me – said you were sore because I got here late.

(*He walks over to her.*)

You're not sore, are you kid?

JEANIE. No.

> (**CHRIS**, **MILTON** *and* **STU** *start to play again.
> A few of the* **BOYS** *and* **GIRLS** *start to slip
> easily into some light jazz steps – but this is
> all done upstage of the piano.)*

BOB. Know what made me late? I was lookin' at that piano.

> (**JEANIE** *stops and turns slowly, as if unable
> to resist talking about the piano.)*

JEANIE. The one I told you about?

BOB. Ueh. On fifty-seventh street. The little one.

> *(Pause.)*

JEANIE. Did you like it?

BOB. Sure did. Wish I could buy it for you. Maybe by Christmas I can save enough for a down payment, huh?

JEANIE. What were you and Sidney fighting about?

BOB. We weren't fighting. We were just clowning... weren't we, Sid?

SIDNEY. *(Working on his lamp.)* Yeh. Just clowning.

> *(A few members of the* **COMPANY** *come on up
> left.)*

HERBIE. Ain't that crazy.

BOB. *(Lowering his voice to* **JEANIE**.*)* Come here. I want to tell you something.

> *(He lifts her on to the Stage Manager's desk.)*

LARRY. *(Enter upstage right with clipboard/pencil.)* Hey, Sidney, we've got to get this bridge out of the way. People will be coming in and knocking the lamps off... their angles.

(He stops in the middle of his sentence because he has looked over and seen **JEANIE** *sitting on the desk talking to* **BOB***.)*

HERBIE. *(Coming over to him.)* Hi, Larry. Did you hear what I'm going to do for these kids? I'm going to get them a chance with Arthur Godfrey. When I get on the air would you like me to give you a plug? Like I can say we got an Assistant Stage Manager who's one great guy?

LARRY. Excuse me a minute, Herbie.

(Then he goes over to the desk.)

Bob. I'm afraid I've got to get at my desk. I've got some work.

BOB. Okay. This is your desk.

(Picking up **JEANIE.***)*

And this is my girl.

*(***BOB*** exits with* **JEANIE.***)*

[MUSIC 04 – "THAT'S THE WAY THAT IT HAPPENS" (REPRISE)]

(The kids start to dance to **CHRIS, MILTON** *and* **STU***'s music, but it is soft and the dancing does not get hot yet. The lights come down to a pleasing glow on the dancers who group around the piano, swaying in rhythm.* **LARRY** *at his desk, is in a spot just as* **JEANIE** *was when she sang.)*

LARRY. *(Puts pad on desk – singing.)*
YOU'RE A GUY IN NEW HAVEN, ON THE ROAD WITH A
    SHOW.
THERE'S A GIRL IN THE COMP'NY,
THAT YOU HARDLY KNOW.

YOU WATCH HER AND YOU WONDER
IF SHE'D LIKE TO PARTAKE
OF FRENCH FRIED POTATOES AND A T-BONE STEAK.

(He looks off left again.)

THEN ALONG COMES A FELLOW
WHO IS QUICKER THAN YOU,
AND HE DOES WHAT YOU THOUGHT
THAT YOU WOULD LIKE TO DO –
HE TAKES HER TO A BISTRO
WHERE THEY GIVE YOU A BREAK
WITH FRENCH FRIED POTATOES AND A T-BONE STEAK.

(Cross to ladder – leans on it.)

NOW YOU SEE THEM TOGETHER AND YOU KNOW IN YOUR
    HEART
THAT YOU LOST WHAT YOU WANTED AT THE VERY START,
BECAUSE YOU DIDN'T ASK HER IF SHE'D LIKE TO PARTAKE
OF FRENCH FRIED POTATOES AND A T-BONE STEAK.

(Move two steps right.)

THAT'S THE WAY IT HAPPENS,
THAT'S THE WAY IT HAPPENS,
THAT'S THE WAY IT HAPPENED TO ME!

(Move to desk – writes on pad.)

SIDNEY. Hey Ernie! Take the bridge up a little.

*(**LARRY** sits at desk. He looks offstage again. The spot fades down again on him and the lights come up on the dancing group. **FRANCINE** pleads with **GEORGE** to start the whistle, which he does, and we go into the dance, building it to a big climax. After applause it is started again and after about sixteen measures, **MAC** enters.)*

MAC. Two minutes after Larry!

LARRY. *(Rises – goes on stage side of desk.)* Hey George, see if they're all signed in?

GEORGE. *(Calls.)* Fifteen minutes – fifteen minutes.

> *(Meanwhile **MAC** turns to the rest of the **COMPANY** who are melting away very quickly. He calls to the last girl going out.)*

MAC. Monica!

> *(**MONICA** turns and tries to look casual.)*

I see you've been down to the beach.

MONICA. *(Assuming gay and girlish innocence.)* How do you like my sunburn?

MAC. Great! Just dandy. Best way I know to take the audience's mind off a play.

> *(She opens her mouth to answer but closes it again.)*

Sometimes a girl dances so much better than all the others that she stands out like a sore thumb. You've got a different way. You try to <u>look</u> like a sore thumb!

> *(She looks down at herself to check.)*

Go and get dressed.

MONICA. *(Somebody touches her back.)* OUCH!

> *(She exits.)*

MAC. *(Indicates the paper on the desk.)* Let's have a look at the report.

> *(**LARRY** hands it to him.)*

> *(He starts to read it.)*

We ran three minutes longer last night.

LARRY. Yes. Lost one minute on intermission.

(**RUBY**, *the company manager, enters.*)

RUBY. Herbie, I'm only the company manager, but...

(**HERBIE** *starts, then turns back to* **RUBY**.)

HERBIE. *(To* **RUBY**.) Hey Ruby have you heard, I'm sponsoring an act on the Arthur Godfrey show?

RUBY. If Mr. Shubert drops in and sees nobody behind your candy counter, who's going to sponsor you?

HERBIE. Oh my gosh!

(*He exits.*)

MAC. *(His eyes still on the Stage Manager's report, pretending to read it while he speaks. During the ensuing scene the crew are setting up the scenery and props for the first scene of* "Me and Juliet".) That was quite a clambake going on when I came in here.

LARRY. I guess I should have stopped it. They were all having such a good time that I –

MAC. Well let them have a good time after the show. I don't care –

GIRL. *(Running across stage.)* I'm awfully sorry the traffic was terrible.

(*He becomes conscious that* **MAC** *has looked up from the report and is studying him.*)

LARRY. I suppose you're thinking I'll never make a good Stage Manager.

MAC. *(After a pause.)* Is that what you want to be?

LARRY. Why, yes. I guess so. Sure.

MAC. What you really want to be is a director, isn't it?

LARRY. Yes, but I ought to learn to run a stage first.

MAC. Not necessarily. Lots of good directors were lousy Stage Managers. Josh Logan was lousy Stage Manager.

LARRY. That's encouraging.

(Hangs up clipboard.)

MAC. Stage managing is a special kind of job, like directing or acting or anything else. The Stage Manager is like the mayor of a small town, He's got to –

CHARLIE CLAY. *(From offstage.)* Mac!

Mac!

*(**LARRY** moves down right.)*

*(**CHARLIE** enters left in a dressing gown and crosses to them, fuming.)*

*(Hearing the note in **CHARLIE**'s voice, **MAC** winces and turns to meet the onslaught.)*

(Quietly.)

Mac, I don't want to pull any corny temperament... but has an actor got the right to have the audience hear him when he sings? ...Does the audience come to hear him? –

(He starts to raise his voice.)

– or do they come to hear a lot of trombones and drums. Just tell me! I want to know!

(He is now screeching.)

That idiot! That conductor –!

MAC. I'll talk to Dario.

CHARLIE. Well, damn it, if you don't –

LARRY. Here's Dario. Take it easy.

(Move in below **MAC**.*)*

(Following his eyes, **MAC** *and* **CHARLIE** *turn and see* **DARIO**, *who has just entered left.*

He is wearing a dinner coat. He carries a small square cardboard box, which he puts on the piano. During the ensuing dialogue he opens it.)

CHARLIE. *(Lowering his voice tactfully.)* Well, tell him.

MAC. I'll tell him.

CHARLIE. *(Move above desk. Still whispering, but through his teeth.)* Because if he does it to me again tonight, I'm going downstairs and wait outside the pit, and when he comes out I'm going to punch him right in the nose.

MAC. I'll tell him.

> *(***CHARLIE** *turns and crosses left of the stage. As he passes him,* **DARIO** *looks up.)*

DARIO. *(He is just taking a gardenia out of the box.)* Good evening, Charlie.

CHARLIE. *(With friendly heartiness.)* Hi ya, Dario baby!

> *(***CHARLIE** *exits,* **MAC***'s eyes following him off as he muses.)*

MAC. Lovable Charlie Clay! Audiences adore him – they say he's got a wistful quality.

LARRY. *(Nodding towards* **DARIO**.*)* Is it true that Dario is leaving the show?

MAC. He <u>thinks</u> he's leaving. But he's the best conductor in town and I'm not going to let him go.

LARRY. How're you going to get him to stay if he doesn't want to?

MAC. I got a gimmick.

> (*Looking across speculatively at* **DARIO** *who has taken a letter from the box and is reading it.*)

See that letter he's reading? It's from a dame who signs herself "the gardenia lady" – says she's crazy about him, and that she'll be somewhere in the audience tonight.

LARRY. How do you know what's in the letter?

MAC. I wrote it.

> (**DARIO** *having read the letter, folds it tenderly and puts it in his breast pocket. With a soulful smile he puts the gardenia in his lapel.*)

I'm going to send him one every night. I figure he won't leave the show till he finds out who the dame is.

> (**DARIO** *pins on flower as he crosses center stage.*)

> (*By this time, Scene One of* "ME AND JULIET" *has been nearly set. It is, of course, off center at the moment – and the* **COMPANY** *are drifting on to the stage and taking their places. The dancers, as usual, are stretching and limbering up.*)

DARIO. (*Crossing to* **MAC** *and* **LARRY** *walking on a cloud.*) Good evening, gentlemen. Is it time for me to go in yet?

MAC. Just about.

> (**DARIO** *turns and starts to exit, humming happily.*)

> (**LARRY** *sits at the desk.*)

> (**MAC** *calls to* **DARIO.**)

Oh, Dario!

>   (*The* **FIRST MEMBERS** *of the company in costume come on.*)

>   (**DARIO** *turns.*)

Charlie says –

DARIO. Ooh! I know! I am drowning him out! Every night the same.

>   (*Starting to work himself up into a temper something like* **CHARLIE**'s.)

Tell him for me that thirty people in an orchestra can play no quieter!

MAC. Well, he's got a cold. Got a bum throat.

DARIO. (*Raising his voice.*) He was born with a bum throat. That man is my only reason for leaving the show. You know that!

MAC. (*Pointing at the gardenia, tactfully changing the subject.*) No carnation tonight?

DARIO. (*Immediately brought back to heaven, looking down at his lapel.*) No. I thought I would wear a gardenia tonight.

>   (*He smiles with serene contentment.*)

>   (**GEORGE**, *crosses the stage to* **MAC**.)

GEORGE. (*Enter down left exits up left.*) OK Mac, I've sent the men in.

DARIO. Good. I shall go down. Funny thing. I just feel like playing the show tonight.

>   (*He turns and starts to sing happily as he exits through the wings.*)

(Some stage hands move the Juliet balcony to a mark left center.)

MAC. *(To* LARRY.*)* I think this is going to work. I want to go out front for the overture.

(Crosses right.)

Want to see what happens when Dario goes into the orchestra pit. I bet he'll get dizzy looking around for the dame.

(Cross right centre.)

*(*MAC *starts off. More of the company keep coming on.* LILY, *who plays* JULIET, *calls after him.)*

LILY. *(Entering right.)* Oh Mac. I've arranged with the office to take my vacation in August.

MAC. *(Starts to exit.)* Okay, Lily. Have a good time.

(Sees two GIRLS *sitting on chairs.)*

Get up off those costumes.

(Exits.)

*(*LARRY *moves down center. Having heard this, he looks around for* JEANIE, *who happens to be nearby. He catches her eye and calls to her shyly.)*

LARRY. Jeanie.

(He walks over to her.)

I wanted to ask you something. When Lily takes her vacation in August, her understudy will have to go on.

*(*JEANIE *moves down center. She looks at him steadily, waiting for him to finish his story.)*

(This disconcerts **LARRY** *and he stutters and stumbles a bit.)*

You know, in the summertime, when understudies cover principals, we've got to get other understudies to – er – cover them.

JEANIE. Gee Larry, I don't think I'd even have the nerve to go on. I don't want to be an actress. The only reason I tried to get in this show was because the pay was good.

LARRY. The pay'll be fifteen dollars a week more if you make second understudy.

JEANIE. Me play Juliet. I don't think I'm the Juliet type.

LARRY. I think you are. Help you buy that piano.

JEANIE. How did you know –?

LARRY. About the piano? You told me once. You said you knew just where you'd put it – between two windows in your room.

JEANIE. Imagine your remembering that!

*(***LARRY*** *crosses to desk.)*

LARRY. Overture!

(Laugh **CHARLIE** *and* **GIRLS.** **JEANIE** *follows.)*

(Into the microphone.) Everybody in first scene – places on stage!

SIDNEY. Ernie, let her in!

JEANIE. I can't understand how that happened to stick in your mind – about me saving up for a piano. How did you happen to remember that?

LARRY. I remembered it. Thought about it often.

BOB. Here we go, kid.

LARRY. *(Into the microphone.)* Overture! Everybody in first scene! Overture!

(At this point the bridge is lowered from the flies.)

BOY A. *(Walking up to a* GIRL.*)* Can I have some of your mascara?

GIRL B. Sure.

(He takes some mascara off her eyelash, between his thumb and forefinger.)

BOY A. Got a hole in my tights.

(The BOY *rubs the black mascara on his leg to cover up the hole. This is all done with the laconic resourcefulness of professionals. No comment.)*

SIDNEY. Take it away.

(The bridge is raised slowly. The "ME AND JULIET" curtain is lowered in front of it, but it is transparent while the lights remain on behind it. Therefore you can see the bridge being raised with its colored lights glowing. On the stage the singers start to warm up with scales and exercises. The dancers limber up and stretch. JEANIE *waves to* BOB *as the bridge goes up and then she looks over at* LARRY. *As the curtain hits the stage the lights are taken off behind it and it is no longer transparent.)*

Scene Two: The Orchestra Pit

(The lights flood the show-curtain of "ME AND JULIET". Then a spot hits **DARIO** *entering the pit. As he mounts the stand he gazes around the audience, obviously trying to spot the lady of the gardenia. He taps the stand and starts the overture.)*

[MUSIC 05 - "OVERTURE TO ME AND JULIET (DARIO'S OVERTURE)"]

(For a while he concentrates on the music. Then, at a sentimental part, he turns around again and takes a chance that the lady of the gardenia is watching him. He lowers his nose and smells the gardenia passionately. He goes back to conducting, then as the orchestra starts to build to its climax, he looks around to make sure she is watching his magnificent gyrations. After he brings his baton down on the last beat of the overture, he turns and takes a bow and takes advantage of the bowing to look again for his "lady of the gardenia" and to blew a kiss at her, wherever she may be. Then he turns, lifts his baton, and brings it down to start the short prelude which will bring the curtain up on "ME AND JULIET".)

(Scrim and teaser up.)

Scene Three: Prologue

[MUSIC 06 – "OPENING OF ME AND JULIET (PROLOGUE)"]

GIRLS.
WHERE IS THIS?

JULIET.
IT DOESN'T MATTER,
THE SCENE OF THE PLAY
IS NEITHER HERE NOR THERE.
ALL THE THINGS
ABOUT TO HAPPEN
ARE THINGS THAT ARE ALWAYS HAPPENING EV'RYWHERE.

GIRLS.
WHEN IS THIS?

JULIET.
IT DOESN'T MATTER,
THE TIME OF THE PLAY
IS NEITHER NOW NOR THEN.
EV'RY YEAR
THE WORLD IS CHANGING
BUT WOMEN REMAIN THE SAME –

(As two spots hit them.)

AND SO DO MEN!

CHORUS. *(Speaking in rhythm.)*
WHO ARE THEY?

ME. They are the most important people in my life.

(Move downstage.)

CHORUS. *(Speaking in rhythm.)*
WHO ARE YOU?

ME.   I? I AM ME. I am an ordinary character, with an extraordinary interest in myself. My own conception of ME –

> *(He looks at his clothes.)*

Is – er – idealized. The things that happen to ME seem remarkable. The people I know – well look at them!

> *(Indicating Don Juan.)*

This man here, is my boss.

> *(Move downstage.)*

His name is Emil Phlugfelder. But he has so many girls chasing him. That I call him – DON JUAN. That is how I see him – as Don Juan!

> *(Back down right.)*

> *(**DON JUAN** comes to life and the **GIRLS** dance with him until his exit with the **GIRLS**.)*

> *(After **DON JUAN**'s exit.)*

On the mezzanine floor

> *(Cross down center.)*

Of the place where I work there's a girl – one of the file clerks.

> *(He turns towards **JULIET**.)*

I look up from my desk and there she is, on the balcony. I always see her in a kind of glow. To me, she is – JULIET! She's the girl I'm going to marry.

> *(Cross center toward **CARMEN**.)*

This one is a girl. I am <u>not</u> going to marry ... But she <u>bothers</u> me.

(Cross down right.)

I see her everywhere –in the subway, in the park, on the beach. I call her – CARMEN.

(Cross left center.)

*(**CARMEN** dance.)*

*(After **CARMEN** and dancers exit.)*

Now you know them all, the characters who will shape my life. But this one

*(Indicating **JULIET**.)*

My life didn't really begin till I met her. I'll never forget our first date. We sat on a park bench and fed the pigeons! Ah, Juliet! Look at her! So young, so in need of protection. As soon as you see a girl like that. You want to marry her, so that you can protect her

From all the men

Who want to protect her from you!

(He looks back at her.)

She makes me think of gentle and beautiful things: Sunlit meadows, the laughter of children.

Juliet!
(She turns to him and smiles.)

(He turns to audience.)

When she speaks, it is like the faint echo of far-off bells on a misty morning.

*(He turns back to **JULIET**.)*

Speak to me, Juliet!

JULIET. Hi!

(**ME** *sighs ecstatically.*)

[MUSIC 07 – "MARRIAGE TYPE LOVE"]

ME. *(He sings.)*
WHEN FIRST I LAID MY LONGING EYES ON YOU,
I SAW MY FUTURE SHINING IN YOUR FACE,
AND WHEN YOU SMILED AND MURMURED
"HOW D'YOU DO?!"
THE ROOM BECAME A DREAM-ENCHANTED PLACE.

(Now a new rhythm with sharper accent.)
THE CHANDELIERS WERE SHOOTING STARS,
THE DRUMS AND HORNS AND SOFT GUITARS
WERE SOUNDING MORE LIKE NIGHTINGALES,
THE WINDOW CURTAINS BLEW LIKE SAILS,
AND I WAS FLOATING JUST ABOVE THE FLOOR
FEELING SLIGHTLY TALLER THAN BEFORE.

OUT OF NOWHERE
CAME THE FEELING,
KNEW THE FEELING –
MARRIAGE TYPE LOVE.

WE WERE DANCING
AND YOUR EYELASH
BLINKED ON MY LASH –
MARRIAGE TYPE LOVE!

WE MADE A DATE, COULDN'T WAIT
FOR MY DAY OFF.
NOW IT'S A THING WITH A RING
FOR THE PAY-OFF!

I'M YOUR PIGEON,
THROUGH WITH ROAMING,
I AM HOMING
TO MARRIAGE TYPE LOVE AND YOU.

(The chorus joins them in singing.)

GIRLS. *(Humming.)*

AH

AH

GIRLS & BOYS.

OUT OF NOWHERE

CAME THE FEELING,

KNEW THE FEELING –

MARRIAGE TYPE LOVE.

WE WERE DANCING

AND YOUR EYELASH

BLINKED ON MY LASH –

MARRIAGE TYPE LOVE!

JULIET.

WE MADE A DATE, COULDN'T WAIT

FOR MY DAY OFF.

ME.

NOW IT'S A THING WITH A RING

FOR THE PAY-OFF!

BOYS.	**GIRLS.** *(Humming.)*
I'M YOUR PIGEON,	HM, PIGEON
THROUGH WITH ROAMING,	HM, ROAMING
I AM HOMING	HM, HOMING

GIRLS & BOYS.

TO MARRIAGE TYPE LOVE

MARRIAGE TYPE LOVE

MARRIAGE TYPE LOVE AND YOU.

(As the curtain comes down on this prologue to "ME AND JULIET", CHARLIE as ME and LILY as JULIET step forward so that the curtain is behind them.)

[MUSIC 08 - "MARRIAGE TYPE LOVE (ENCORE)"]

(They sing an encore refrain during which DARIO makes the orchestra play very loudly and drown CHARLIE out every time he sings. When JULIET sings he plays softly.)

JULIET.
OUT OF NOWHERE
CAME THE FEELING,
KNEW THE FEELING –
MARRIAGE TYPE LOVE.

ME. *(Drowned out by orchestra.)*
WE WERE DANCING
AND YOUR EYELASH
BLINKED ON MY LASH –
MARRIAGE TYPE LOVE!

JULIET.
WE MADE A DATE, COULDN'T WAIT
FOR YOUR DAY OFF.
NOW IT'S A THING WITH A RING
FOR THE PAY-OFF!

ME. *(Drowned out again.)*
I'M YOUR PIGEON,
THROUGH WITH ROAMING,
I AM HOMING

ME & JULIET.
TO MARRIAGE TYPE LOVE AND YOU.

*(As the refrain is ended **JULIET** blows a kiss to **DARIO** as she exits, **CHARLIE** infuriated mutters something which if you can read lips is very insulting indeed. Scowling at **DARIO**, he makes his exit.)*

[MUSIC 09 – "CHANGE OF SCENE"]

Scene Four: The Light Bridge

(Presumably hanging at its proper level in the flies, the light bridge is actually about nine feet above stage level. A black, neutral drop hangs behind it.)

(BOB and SIDNEY are busily changing colors in their lamps.)

SIDNEY. *(Continuing on argument.)* All right, so I'm stupid! I still say I don't know what the hell it's about.

(Cross to BOB.)

First thing that happens, a dame comes out and tells the audience the scene is no place and the time is any time at all. If they don't know where the hell they are, how are the audience going to know?

(SIDNEY crosses right.)

BOB. It's symbolic. This guy they call "Me". He's the kind that wants a wife and a couple of kids and a little house somewhere... Flushing or some place like that.

(The music changes as if a new scene has started below.)

SIDNEY. Flushing, huh? I don't live so far from there.

BOB. That's what I mean.

SIDNEY. You mean I'm like him?

BOB. In a general way.

SIDNEY. *(Derisively.)* Ah, go on! Do you think I'd be acting like he's acting now. Look at him down there! Sitting on a park bench!

*(They both look down. Seductive music, a
new strain is coming up from below.)*

That Carmen giving him the business and him looking
like a scared rabbit – Look at her! Rollin' her eyes at
him.

BOB. Boy, she's rolling everything! You can see good from
up here... Did y'ever think what fun it'd be to stand up
here and drop sandbags on the actors? Pick 'em off one
by one –

SIDNEY. Look at that guy now! Why don't he give in to
that Carmen dame?

BOB. He's got the other one on his mind. Don't you see
she's in a vision back there. He sees Juliet in his dreams
while Carmen is trying to make him. When a guy
makes up his mind to marry, he doesn't want to look at
any outside stuff – for a while. Didn't you feel like that
before you got married?

*(**SIDNEY** thinks.)*

Well, didn't you?

SIDNEY. I'm just trying to remember, The way I proposed
to Josephine was kinda funny. All her family were
there, her mother and her father and three brothers.
And the oldest brother said: "When are you kids going
to get married?" And everybody looked at me, and
I said: "Oh, whenever Josephine will have me". You
know, I was kinda half jokin'... five minutes later all the
neighbors came in and we were havin' drinks and that's
what they called announcing the engagement.

BOB. Well, you loved her, didn't you?

SIDNEY. Sure I loved her.

BOB. So you see, the other dames couldn't tempt you...
Could they?

(Pause.)

SIDNEY. How do I know? Nobody tried!

[MUSIC 10 – "SCENE ON LIGHT BRIDGE"]

Nobody like that Carmen down there.

> (**BOB** *looks down. The refrain of* ["KEEP IT GAY"] *is being played.)*

BOB. *(Still looking down.)* This Don Juan feller, he's more like me. We like a good time.

SIDNEY. Aw, so do I like a good time.

BOB. *(Laughing.)* Sure you do. You <u>like</u> it, but you don't <u>get</u> it.

> (**BOB** *sings with the music:)*

LA LA LA LA LA LA
LA LA LA LA LA LA
LET IT SING LIKE A NIGHTINGALE IN MAY,
KEEP IT GAY –

SIDNEY. *(In a loud whisper.)* Sh! They'll hear you down there!

BOB. They can't hear me.

> *(Singing.)*

TAKE IT EASY AND ENJOY IT WHILE YOU TAKE IT!

SIDNEY. If you like singing so much why don't you get a job as an actor?

BOB. I bet I could play the part better than the mug who's playing it now.

[MUSIC 11 – "KEEP IT GAY"]

WHEN A GIRL WOULD MEET DON JUAN
SHE'D GET GOOFY FOR THE DON.
LIKE A SNAKE WHO MEETS A MONGOOSE,

THAT YOUNG LADY WAS A GONE GOOSE.

ANY TIME A GIRL WOULD SAY:

"SHALL WE NAME A WEDDING DAY?"

JUAN WOULD TRY ANOTHER GAMBIT

HE LIKED WEDDINGS NOT A DAMN BIT.

HE WOULD GAZE INTO THE LADY'S EYE,

STRUMMING HIS GUITAR TO STALL FOR TIME.

THEN HE'D MAKE HIS USUAL REPLY –

THAT OLD RELIABLE ANDALUSIAN RHYME:

KEEP IT GAY, KEEP IT LIGHT,

KEEP IT FRESH, KEEP IT FAIR.

LET IT BLOOM EV'RY NIGHT,

GIVE IT ROOM, GIVE IT AIR!

KEEP YOUR LOVE A LOVELY DREAM AND NEVER WAKE IT!

MAKE IT HAPPY AND BE HAPPY AS YOU MAKE IT!

LET IT SING LIKE A NIGHTINGALE IN MAY

KEEP IT GAY, KEEP IT FREE

OR YOU'LL FRIGHTEN IT AWAY.

TAKE IT EASY AND ENJOY IT WHILE YOU TAKE IT!

KEEP IT GAY,

KEEP IT GAY,

KEEP IT GAY!

(The lights go out on the bridge. The bridge and its drop are taken away while light is concentrated on the lower part of the stage. The small center picture now broadens out on both sides of the stage so the whole company can be seen dancing in the performance of "ME AND JULIET".)

[MUSIC 12 - "KEEP IT GAY (DANCE)"]

CHORUS.

KEEP IT GAY, KEEP IT LIGHT,

KEEP IT FRESH, KEEP IT FAIR.

LET IT BLOOM EV'RY NIGHT,

GIVE IT ROOM, GIVE IT AIR!
KEEP YOUR LOVE A LOVELY DREAM AND NEVER WAKE IT.
MAKE IT HAPPY AND BE HAPPY AS YOU MAKE IT!
LET IT SING LIKE A NIGHTINGALE IN MAY
KEEP IT GAY, KEEP IT FREE
OR YOU'LL FRIGHTEN IT AWAY.
TAKE IT EASY AND ENJOY IT WHILE YOU TAKE IT!
KEEP IT GAY,
KEEP IT GAY,
KEEP IT GAY!

(The stage is blacked out for only a few seconds, during which we blend into the next scene. During the five seconds while it is dark, the orchestra is succeeded by a rehearsal piano.)

Scene Five: The Stage

[MUSIC 13 – "SCENE 5"]

(The lights come up, finding **DON JUAN** *and the chorus continuing the same number in the same grouping in which we left them, except that now the whole company is in practice clothes.)*

*(***CHRIS** *is playing piano for rehearsal over at the right side of the stage.* **RUBY** *leans on the piano, just sort of "hanging around, watching things".* **LARRY** *stands against the proscenium.)*

(Behind them are flats and drops from the production of "ME AND JULIET". Around the traveller curtains, on either side, are wooden rails to protect them, and "pants" of burlap around them, as there were in Scene One.)

CHORUS
> KEEP IT GAY,
> KEEP IT GAY,
> KEEP IT GAY.

(After the dance **MAC***'s voice can be heard.)*

MAC'S VOICE. *(On microphone.)* All right, all right! That was fine! Now we've got it back to the way we had it!

(The **COMPANY** *stand, sit and lie on the stage, panting heavily, looking out front, listening to* **MAC***, as if he were making a speech from about the tenth row. They seem faintly embarrassed, as all groups do when*

listening to a speech from a Stage Manager or producer.)

I know it's no fun rehearsing on a hot day in June, but it's also no fun to be out of a job on a cold day in February, and that's what'll happen to all of us if we don't keep these performances up. OK that's all. Thank you.

(The group breaks up and drifts offstage, some quickly, others slowly. **SIDNEY** *comes down to the very edge of the stage and peers out into the dark auditorium.)*

SIDNEY. Hey, Mac! Can I have the stage now?

MAC'S VOICE. *(From the front.)* Not right away. We've got replacement auditions for the part of Carmen. You can have it in about twenty minutes.

LARRY. *(Cross center. Coming down quickly.)* I've got an understudy call right after the audition.

SIDNEY. *(Cross center.)* Then when the hell am I going to get a chance to change my color frames?

(Talking out to **MAC.**)

All the colors are faded. You were complaining last night.

MAC'S VOICE. Who are you rehearsing, Larry?

LARRY. Second understudy for Juliet, I'm trying out Jeanie.

(There is a pause.)

MAC'S VOICE. *(From the front.)* Oh... Well, hold it a minute. I'll come up on stage and we'll talk it over.

*(***LARRY*** *turns to* **SIDNEY,** *in the manner of one making a retreat.)*

LARRY. I think we can work it out all right, Sidney. I'll rehearse downstage here, if you'll try not to make a lot of noise while you're –

(*Both cross up left. Smiling as if he knows a secret.*)

SIDNEY. I'll be quiet as a little mouse, chum. I wouldn't interfere with your – rehearsal – for anything in the world.

(*Both cross upstage.* **SIDNEY** *exits across the other side of the stage.*)

CHRIS. (*To* **RUBY**.) What's that about replacement auditions for Carmen?

RUBY. We've got to get a new one. Susie's leaving. She's going to have a baby.

CHRIS. Susie?

RUBY. Ask Susie's husband.

GIRL. Jim?

DON JUAN. Yes I am – I mean she is.

MAC. (*Entering, making a general announcement to all the stragglers.*) Clear the stage! We're having auditions here in a minute. What are you hanging around for?

LARRY. Oh, Mac. I fixed it with Sidney. He can lower the number nine pipe and I'll work downstage here.

MAC. (*Preoccupied with other thoughts.*) Fine... Fine.

(*He looks at* **LARRY** *as if studying him.*)

LARRY. Didn't I tell you I was going to try Jeanie out? I think maybe she'd be a good cover for Lily's understudy... Don't you?

MAC. Larry, step over here for a minute, will you?

(He leads him over left proscenium.)

There's one rule I never broke in my life. And it'd be a good idea if no Stage Manager ever broke it.

LARRY. What's that?

MAC. *(Speaking slowly.)* Don't ever let yourself get stuck on anybody that works in the same company as you do.

LARRY. I'm not stuck on anybody in this company.

MAC. Well, good. I'm glad to hear it. Because there's nothing worse for busting a troupe wide open.

LARRY. *(A little impatiently.)* Well, I told you, I'm not –

MAC. If it ever happened to me, I'd fire the girl – or quit the show myself. I wouldn't compromise one inch!

LARRY. *(Testily.)* OK, OK I get it.

MAC. *(Move right of* **LARRY.***)* There are plenty of cute kids in the other shows around town.

> *(Trying to take the edge off now, and lighten the whole scene. He leans over and taps* **LARRY** *on the arm.)*

As a matter of fact, I'm working on some new talent myself right now. You know little Betty Loraine.

LARRY. Betty Loraine – with the show across the street?

MAC. That's the one. Funny little thing. Never seems to wear anything but dungarees and sweaters, things like that. I'm just beginning to spar with her. Last night –

RUBY. *(Move down center. Calling across stage.)* Hey, Mac! Here's Mr. Harrison!

> *(Waving out towards back of theatre.)*

How <u>are</u> you, Mr. Harrison? Enjoy your vacation?

HARRISON'S VOICE. *(On microphone. From out front – loudspeaker in balcony rail.)* Not much. I'm glad to be home. Are you ready for me, Mac?

MAC. *(Center.)* Right away, Mr. Harrison. Got two replacement candidates here. They're getting into their practice clothes.

(Turning.)

See if they're ready, Larry.

*(**LARRY** exits.)*

MISS DAVENPORT'S VOICE. *(Front out front.)* Hello, Mac.

*(**LARRY** up to get chairs up left.)*

MAC. *(Peering out into the darkness.)* Who's that?

HARRISON'S VOICE. I've got Miss Davenport with me.

MAC. Swell! Good to see you, Miss Davenport.

HARRISON'S VOICE. She's really here to protect her choreography – Afraid you and I might take a girl with a wooden leg.

MAC. *(He does his best to laugh convincingly at what obviously he considers a bad joke.)* The first girl I'm going to show you was with Ballet Theatre.

(Move upstage left.)

DAVENPORT'S VOICE. What's her name?

MAC. Hilda Morton.

DAVENPORT'S VOICE. Oh, I know her.

(Lowering her voice.)

She's a very good dancer, Ben.

*(**HILDA** enters.)*

There she is, coming on now.

HARRISON'S VOICE.   *(Also in low tones.)* She's not a Carmen type.

MAC. *(Leading* HILDA *forward.)* Mr. Harrison, this is Miss Morton.

HARRISON'S VOICE.   How do you do?

HILDA.   *(Peering out into the dark auditorium.)* I'm awfully glad to know you, Mr. Harrison. Hello, Miss Davenport.

DAVENPORT'S VOICE.   Hello, Hilda. Start with some tour jetés.

> *(*HILDA *moves up, looking above her to make sure she is up above the light. Then she starts to dance and she does the steps beautifully.)*

Fine. Now a grand jeté.

> *(*HILDA *obliges expertly.)*

HARRISON'S VOICE.   *(In a dry and final voice.)* Thank you very much, Miss Morton.

> *(*HILDA, *knowing that is her dismissal, bows and smiles mechanically and starts offstage.)*

DAVENPORT'S VOICE.   Wait a minute. Just a moment, Hilda.

> *(*HILDA *lingers. There are sounds of mumbled conversation.)*

I know she can dance the part.

HARRISON'S VOICE.   She can't look it.

> *(Then louder, in a weary, resigned voice.)*

All right. Thank you very much, Hilda.

(**SIDNEY** *crosses from right to left. Now* **LARRY** *immediately brings forth another* **GIRL** *and* **MAC** *introduces her.*)

MAC. This is Marcia Laval, Mr. Harrison, Miss Davenport.

HARRISON'S VOICE. Hello, Marcia. How've you been?

MARCIA. *(Delighted to be recognized by the manager.)* Just fine. How are you, Mr. Harrison? I didn't think you'd remember me.

HARRISON'S VOICE. Of course I remember you.

DAVENPORT'S VOICE. *(Sounding skeptical.)* Can you do a tour jeté?

(**MARCIA** *tries and is apparently much more of a show girl than a dancer.*)

MARCIA. Would you like to see my elevation?

DAVENPORT'S VOICE. No. That will do. Thank you very much.

HARRISON'S VOICE. Wait a minute!

(Then again there is mumbled conversation.)

I like this girl.

DAVENPORT'S VOICE. *(Soto voce.)* No certainly not.

HARRISON'S VOICE. *(Disgruntled. Then in a weary voice, louder.)* All right. leave your name with the office so we know where to get in touch with you.

MARCIA. Oh, thank you, Mr. Harrison.

(She goes.)

HARRISON'S VOICE. That all you got, Mac?

MAC. That's all this morning. There's a girl coming in next week from the St. Louis Municipal Opera. They say that she –

> *(He breaks off because he is conscious of*
> **CHARLIE,** *who has just peeked in from the*
> *wings and is waving to* **HARRISON.***)*

CHARLIE. That Ben Harrison out there?

HARRISON'S VOICE. Hello, Charlie.

CHARLIE. *(Coming out on to the stage.)* Have you found a new Carmen for me?

HARRISON'S VOICE. No, we haven't.

CHARLIE. Well I have a young lady with me who I think would be just –

> *(Turning towards wings.)*

Come out here, darling...

> *(***BETTY** *enters. She is as* **MAC** *has described*
> *her, "a funny little thing" in dungarees and*
> *a sweatshirt.)*

> *(***CHARLIE** *takes her by the hand.)*

She's in the show across the street. Miss Betty Loraine... Mr. Harrison, Miss Davenport.

BETTY. *(Beaming at them confidently.)* How do you do?

> *(To* **MAC.***)*

Hello, Charm Boat!

MAC. *(Very formally.)* How do you do, Miss Loraine?

> *(He turns away.)*

> *(***LARRY** *is amused at* **MAC***'s predicament.)*

HARRISON'S VOICE. I'd like to see what you can do. How long would it take you to get into your practice clothes?

BETTY. I <u>am</u> in my practice clothes.

(She takes off her dungarees, under which she wears dancer's tights.)

CHARLIE. Before she dances, would you like to hear her read lines? I got her up in one of the scenes.

*(**LARRY** and **MAC** get chairs.)*

HARRISON'S VOICE. Fine! Go ahead. Say, Mac! It looks as if Charlie's trying to take your job away. Trying to muscle in on you.

MAC. It does look like he's trying to muscle in, doesn't it?

*(**MAC** swings a chair, places it downstage center and sits.)*

BETTY. *(Going over to **MAC**.)* Can I have a script, Mac?

MAC. Certainly, Miss Loraine.

(He hands it to her.)

CHARLIE. *(Sitting on table.)* All right, honey. I'm sitting on a park bench, and you come up to me.

BETTY. *(Reading from script.)* "Why do you pretend not to know I'm alive?"

*(**CHARLIE** looks around at her.)*

"All men know I'm alive. They can't help it, because I <u>am</u> alive!"

(She heaves several deep breaths under her jersey to prove it.)

HARRISON'S VOICE. Fine, fine!

BETTY. *(As **CARMEN**.)* "Why do you sit by yourself in the park reading poetry? Don't you like girls?"

CHARLIE. "Only one – Juliet – and she's an angel – she's too good for me."

BETTY. (*As* **CARMEN.**) "Why don't you see how it feels to be with someone who's not too good for you."

> (**CHARLIE** *lowers his eyes to his imaginary book of poetry.*)

CHARLIE. (*Looking at her.*) "You mean –?"

> (**BETTY** *nods her head vigorously.*)

Oh no. I couldn't!"

BETTY. (*As* **CARMEN.**) "If I thought you couldn't I wouldn't suggest it."

> (*Putting her head on his shoulder. Stepping out of character abruptly, calling out to* **HARRISON.**)

Do you want the number?

HARRISON'S VOICE. Sure!

> (**CHARLIE** *nods to* **CHRIS** *who goes to play the piano.*)

CHARLIE. (*Calling to* **BUZZ** *who is just crossing the stage with an electric guitar and a sound box.*) Buzz! You're just in time!

BUZZ. In time for what?

CHARLIE. Would you do the Keep It Gay routine with this young lady? Like a good fellow?

BUZZ. I got a TV audition at three o'clock –

HARRISON. You've got time, Buzz. Go ahead.

BUZZ. (*Crossly.*) Who's that?

CHARLIE. That's Mr. Harrison.

BUZZ. (*A different man.*) Oh, hello, Mr. Harrison, Sure I've got time. Love to – sure.

CHARLIE. Oh by the way, have you two kids met -- Betty Loraine this is Buzz Miller. She knows the routine, Buzz, OK Chris.

> (**CHRIS** *starts playing.*)

[MUSIC 14 – "THE AUDITION (KEEP IT GAY – REPRISE)"]

BETTY.
> KEEP IT GAY, KEEP IT LIGHT,
> KEEP IT FRESH, KEEP IT FAIR.
> LET IT BLOOM EV'RY NIGHT,
> GIVE IT ROOM, GIVE IT AIR!
> KEEP YOUR LOVE A LOVELY DREAM AND NEVER WAKE IT.
> MAKE IT HAPPY AND BE HAPPY AS YOU MAKE IT!
> LET IT SING LIKE A NIGHTINGALE IN MAY
> KEEP IT GAY, KEEP IT FREE
> OR YOU'LL FRIGHTEN IT AWAY.
> TAKE IT EASY AND ENJOY IT WHILE YOU TAKE IT!
> KEEP IT GAY,
> KEEP IT GAY,
> KEEP IT GAY!

> (*They dance.*)

DAVENPORT'S VOICE. That was fine!

HARRISON'S VOICE. Your show is closing next week, isn't it?

> (*She nods.*)

Send your agent around to see Ruby. Get that, Ruby?

RUBY. Check!

HARRISON. (*To* **BETTY.**) Could you start rehearsing tomorrow?

BETTY. Why not?

HARRISON. Get that, Mac?

MAC. *(Coldly.)* I understand.

HARRISON'S VOICE. Coming over to Sardi's, Charlie?

>*(**MAC** gets up and exits downstage left, taking the chair with him.)*

CHARLIE. Be right with you!

>*(As he passes **BETTY** on his way off.)*

Congratulations!

BETTY. Charlie, you've been wonderful. Thank you.

>*(She gives him a big smacking kiss.)*

>*(**MAC** stamps off the stage. **CHARLIE** exits. **SIDNEY** comes out to the center and calls up to the flies. **BETTY** puts on her dungarees.)*

SIDNEY. Hey, Joe! Let down that number nine pipe, will you?

BETTY. *(Going over to **RUBY**.)* Hey, Ruby – where did Mac go?

>*(**RUBY** shrugs his shoulder and smiles.)*

I don't get it. Last night he was full of sweet talk. Today he acted as if he never met me before.

RUBY. Last night you were a girl in another show. Don't you know about his rule? With any girl in his own company – nothing!

BETTY. Oh, so that's it.

RUBY. You can take this job, or keep Mac... which?

>*(Pause.)*

BETTY. I'm going to take the job! And make him break his rule!

RUBY. You'll be the first girl to turn the trick. "Is he man or machine?" That's what they say about him.

BETTY. If he's a machine I don't want him. If he's a man, I'm going to make him prove it!

(*Meanwhile the number nine pipe has been let down from the flies.* SIDNEY *has brought out a pile of color frames and during the ensuing scene proceeds to change them in the lamps on the pipe.* JEANIE *has come on the stage and she and* LARRY *cross to center.*)

LARRY. Just leave your things right there.

(JEANIE *takes off her hat and places her bag on the upstage chair.*)

Did you get a chance to look over the part?

JEANIE. (*A little guiltily.*) Well, no, Larry. I didn't. I –

LARRY. That's all right. You know all the music, anyway, don't you? Let's start out with one of the songs.

Chris, can you help us out?

CHRIS. (*Nodding.*) What do you want?

LARRY. "No Other Love".

(*To* JEANIE.)

Stand over near the piano, Jeanie.

(JEANIE *looks uncertain.*)

JEANIE. All right – anything you want to tell me first?

LARRY. No. Just go ahead and sing it in your own way.

(JEANIE crosses to the piano. LARRY carries a chair to the center of the stage, straddles it and leans on the back of it, then nods to CHRIS. JEANIE starts to sing. She sings well enough as far as voice is concerned, but her feeling for the lyric is superficial and her gestures are meaningless.)

[MUSIC 15 – "THE AUDITION CONTINUES"]

JEANIE.
NO OTHER LOVE HAVE I,
ONLY MY LOVE FOR YOU,
ONLY THE DREAM–

LARRY. *(Stops her.)* Just a minute, Jeanie.

(He calls over to the piano.)

Chris!

(He waves his hand and CHRIS stops.)

Take five!

(CHRIS exits.)

(There is a pause. LARRY looks at JEANIE as if trying to think of the right words to say. Then he speaks to her quietly.)

Why did you do that just now... with your hands... like this?

(He imitates her gesture.)

JEANIE. I don't know. No reason in particular. I just didn't want to stand like a stick and do nothing.

(Pause.)

LARRY. Suppose you had to describe Juliet – what kind of girl would you say she was?

JEANIE. I'd say she was a nice, ordinary kind of kid.

LARRY. *(Crossing right.)* Do you think Carmen is a stronger character?

JEANIE. Oh, yes... don't you?

LARRY. Jeanie – the whole secret of singing this song is to realize that Juliet is a stronger, deeper, more passionate woman than Carmen.

JEANIE. More passionate?

LARRY. You've seen this happen, Jeanie – two nice, ordinary kids like Juliet and this little guy decide they want to live with each other for the rest of their lives. And suddenly something happens to them – two underdogs are given the strength of giants. They'll knock over anybody who stands in their way.

JEANIE. *(Thoughtfully.)* Yes, I <u>have</u> seen that happen.

LARRY. So has everyone in the audience.

(**JEANIE** *sits.*)

And if you're a real kid like Juliet, they'll recognize you – if you're phony, they'll reject you.

(**LARRY** *moves left.*)

JEANIE. An audience would scare me.

LARRY. Every good actress is scared – scared they won't like her. Her job is to make them like her. And the way to do that is to be honest with them. They're the smartest people in the theatre,

[MUSIC 16 – "THE BIG BLACK GIANT"]

and the toughest, and the nicest.

(Music starts. He starts to sing.)

THE WATER IN A RIVER IS CHANGED EV'RY DAY

AS IT FLOWS FROM THE HILLS TO THE SEA.

(Brings chair down.)

BUT TO PEOPLE ON THE SHORE THE RIVER IS THE SAME,
OR, AT LEAST IT APPEARS TO BE.

(Sit chair left.)

THE AUDIENCE IN A THEATRE IS CHANGED EV'RY NIGHT,
AS A SHOW RUNS ALONG ON ITS WAY.
BUT TO PEOPLE ON THE STAGE THE AUDIENCE LOOKS
   THE SAME,
EV'RY NIGHT, EV'RY MATINEE.
A BIG BLACK GIANT
WHO LOOKS AND LISTENS
WITH THOUSANDS OF EYES AND EARS.
A BIG BLACK MASS
OF LOVE AND PITY
AND TROUBLES AND HOPES AND FEARS;

(Rise.)

AND EV'RY NIGHT
THE MIXTURE'S DIFF'RENT,
ALTHOUGH IT MAY LOOK THE SAME.
TO FEEL HIS WAY
WITH EV'RY MIXTURE
IS PART OF THE ACTOR'S GAME.

(Move right of chair center.)

ONE NIGHT IT'S A LAUGHING GIANT,
ANOTHER NIGHT A WEEPING GIANT.
ONE NIGHT IT'S A COUGHING GIANT,
ANOTHER NIGHT A SLEEPING GIANT.
EV'RY NIGHT YOU FIGHT THE GIANT
AND MAYBE, IF YOU WIN,
YOU SEND HIM OUT A NICER GIANT
THAN HE WAS WHEN HE CAME IN...

(Cross right.)

BUT IF HE DOESN'T LIKE YOU, THEN ALL YOU CAN DO
IS TO PACK UP YOUR MAKE-UP AND GO.
FOR AN ACTOR IN A FLOP THERE ISN'T ANY CHOICE
BUT TO LOOK FOR ANOTHER SHOW.

 (Move right center.)

THAT BIG BLACK GIANT
WHO LOOKS AND LISTENS
WITH THOUSANDS OF EYES AND EARS,
THAT BIG BLACK MASS
OF LOVE AND PITY
AND TROUBLES AND HOPES AND FEARS,
WILL SIT OUT THERE
AND RULE YOUR LIFE
FOR ALL YOUR LIVING YEARS.

 *(After finishing the song **LARRY** turns away. **JEANIE** rises from the chair she has been sitting in and follows him, looking at him with deep interest. **LARRY** turns back to her, a little self-conscious after his long "speech".)*

Now – er – would you like to try the song again? Just remember to be real and... why are you looking at me like that?

JEANIE. *(Flustered.)* Was I –? Oh, excuse me.

LARRY. What's the matter?

JEANIE. Nothing, Larry. I was just thinking – how you can be in the same company with somebody for so long and not really know them at all.

LARRY. *(Move below chair.)* Oh... Shall we try the song now?

 *(Cross **JEANIE**. Calling to **CHRIS**.)*

Chris!

 *(Turning back to **JEANIE**.)*

Now, just think of the girl –

    (Cross left with chair right center.)

out on the balcony, lonely – wishing that the guy would come back.

    (Taking chair and putting it left.)

    (He places it seat toward audience, **JEANIE** *puts her hands on it as on a balcony rail and starts to sing.)*

[MUSIC 17– "NO OTHER LOVE"]

    *(***LARRY*** takes chair downstage left and stops, listening to* **JEANIE** *as she starts to sing in the center of the stage.)*

JEANIE.
NO OTHER LOVE HAVE I,
ONLY MY LOVE FOR YOU,
ONLY THE DREAM WE KNEW
NO OTHER LOVE.
WATCHING THE NIGHT GO BY,
WISHING THAT YOU COULD BE
WATCHING THE NIGHT WITH ME,
INTO THE NIGHT I CRY:
HURRY HOME, COME HOME TO ME!
SET ME FREE,
FREE FROM DOUBT
AND FREE FROM LONGING.
INTO YOUR ARMS I'LL FLY.
LOCKED IN YOUR ARMS I'LL STAY,
WAITING TO HEAR YOU SAY:
NO OTHER LOVE HAVE I,
NO OTHER LOVE.

    *(***LARRY*** rises and goes over to left of* **JEANIE** *and speaks.)*

LARRY. Good. Now try starting it softer then let it build...

> (*To* **CHRIS.**)

Take it half a tone higher.

> (**CHRIS** *plays, and* **LARRY** *starts singing to illustrate.*)

NO OTHER LOVE HAVE I,

LARRY & JEANIE.
> ONLY MY LOVE FOR YOU,

JEANIE.
> ONLY THE DREAM WE KNEW –
> NO OTHER LOVE.
> WATCHING THE NIGHT GO BY

LARRY.
> WATCHING THE NIGHT GO BY

JEANIE.
> WISHING THAT YOU COULD BE

LARRY.
> WISHING THAT YOU COULD BE

JEANIE.
> WATCHING THE NIGHT WITH ME,
> INTO THE NIGHT I CRY:

LARRY.
> HURRY HOME, COME HOME TO ME!
> SET ME FREE.

LARRY & JEANIE.
> FREE FROM DOUBT
> AND FREE

JEANIE.
> FROM LONGING.

LARRY & JEANIE.
> INTO YOUR ARMS I'LL FLY.
> LOCKED IN YOUR ARMS I'LL STAY,
> WAITING TO HEAR YOU SAY:
> NO OTHER LOVE HAVE I,
> NO OTHER LOVE.

> *(After the song, **LARRY** crosses to **CHRIS** at the piano and whispers instructions. **CHRIS** starts to play and **JEANIE** starts the song again in the center of the stage.)*

> *(**BOB** enters at right.)*

JEANIE.
> ONLY THE DREAM WE KNEW,
> NO OTHER LOVE.
> WATCHING THE NIGHT GO BY,
> WISHING THAT YOU COULD BE
> WATCHING THE NIGHT WITH
>   ME,
> INTO THE NIGHT I CRY:

> *(**BOB** watches **JEANIE** singing, signals to **SIDNEY** and walks down stage at the right of **JEANIE** and starts to do a burlesque imitation of her singing.)*

> HURRY HOME, COME HOME –

> *(**JEANIE** stops suddenly, seeing **BOB** imitating her, she turns on him and speaks.)*

What's the matter with you? Making a big joke?

> *(**BOB** squats on floor in front of her, applauds and says.)*

BOB. Encore! Encore!

JEANIE. I don't see anybody laughing.

BOB. *(Cross up right.)* Excuse me for living.

> *(Turn back.)*

I didn't know you were a prima donna from the "Met". I just thought you were one of the girls in the chorus.

(Going upstage to **SIDNEY**.*)*

Want some help, Sid?

SIDNEY. Help me clear these color frames.

*(***BOB*** *picks up a stack of frames and carries them off.)*

JEANIE. *(She crosses to get her hat from chair.)* Do you mind if we stop, Larry?

*(***LARRY*** *crosses left.)*

I'm sorry to be like this. I guess if I was a real actress

I wouldn't let anybody... make any difference.

LARRY. *(Quietly.)* Come down tomorrow and we'll have another shot at it.

*(***GEORGE*** *enters downstage left and crosses upstage right with four chairs.)*

*(***JEANIE*** *starts off.)*

You can go now, Chris. Two o'clock tomorrow.

CHRIS. OK.

(Becoming aware that **LARRY** *is in no mood to talk to anyone,* **CHRIS** *exits.)*

JEANIE. *(Turning at exit.)* Thank you, Larry. Thank you very much.

*(***LARRY*** *smiles and waves.* **JEANIE** *exits up left.)*

SIDNEY. *(Calling. To Flyman.)* Take it away!

LARRY. *(Calling off to* SIDNEY.*)* Will you kill this work light?

VOICE OFFSTAGE. OK.

> *(For some seconds* LARRY *remains rooted to a spot in the center of the stage. The light is switched off. The stage becomes quite dark, except for some shafts of daylight coming from the roof at the back.* LARRY *starts pacing up and down in the dark. This lasts for a few seconds. Then another figure comes on. It must be* BOB, *because it is such a big figure.)*

BOB. Sidney tells me you had quite a rehearsal here.

> *(*LARRY *starts as if shot, and then turns around to face* BOB.*)*

LARRY. *(In a tight voice.)* What do you mean?

BOB. You and Jeanie.

LARRY. Yes, it was fine. I think she'll – she may turn out fine.

> *(He starts to go, but* BOB *reaches forward and grabs him by the arm.)*

BOB. Wait a minute. Don't go yet.

LARRY. Let go of me!

BOB. *(Holding on to his arm.)* What's your hurry? I want to say something to you.

> *(He pulls* LARRY *toward him.)*

> *(The stage is quite dark and the two men can just about be seen.)*

Stand still here a minute and listen to me... Are you making a play for my girl?

LARRY. Of course not!

>(**BOB** *continues to hold him, but says nothing.*)

Let go of me!

>(**LARRY** *tries to break* **BOB***'s hold on him.*)

What's the hell's the matter with you?

>(*There is a stretch of silence.*)

I'm a Stage Manager rehearsing an understudy. What the hell's –

BOB. Just keep it that way, see? Stage Manager and understudy. Strictly business.

>(*His voice becoming even quieter but more threatening.*)

If you ever try to move in on me with that kid, I – I'm just telling you... Something would happen to me... I couldn't <u>help</u> killing you –

[MUSIC 18 – "INCIDENTAL ON DARK STAGE"]

>(*He throws* **LARRY** *away from him and crosses upstage right as he goes.*)

not if I tried...

>(*He exits.*)

>(**LARRY** *stands perfectly still in the darkness, then he starts to pace.* **LARRY** *exits.*)

Scene Six: The Alley Leading to the Stage Door

[MUSIC 19 – "DANCE IN THE ALLEY"]

*(Various members of the company ride on with set, seated on benches, stage door steps, etc. **HERBIE** is among them, reading a copy of Billboard. As the scene moves down, three dancers are improvising steps, keeping ahead of set.)*

*(During the dance **CHARLIE** enters up left and crosses to the stage door, stops and watches the dancers. At the finish of the dance, there is a general ad lib of approval from the boys and girls, and applause. Then a **GIRL** speaks.)*

A GIRL. They ought to have a spot in the show.

CHARLIE. It's easy to perform in an alley. But the only thing that pays off is what you do out there on the stage in front of an audience!

(He exits.)

A BOY. Lovable Charlie Clay.

*(Now **JIM** comes staggering on, pale, his voice quavering.)*

DON JUAN. Hello, everybody.

BOY C. Hi, Jim.

ANOTHER GIRL. How's Susie?

DON JUAN. She's – started!

ANOTHER BOY. The baby.

DON JUAN. She just took me to the hospital. I mean – I wanted to stay but she said I had to come and give the show.

(He exits into stage door.)

ANOTHER BOY. He's white as a sheet –

(He exits into stage door.)

GIRL. It seems only yesterday when Susie left the show.

A GIRL. I wish I had a baby.

A BOY. You do?

A GIRL. *(Looking at him coldly.)* I mean legitimate.

A BOY. Oh.

(**TWO GIRLS** *enter, followed by* **HERBIE.**)

(**LILY** *enters and crosses toward stage door.)*

HERBIE. Hi, Lily! How'd you make out?

LILY. I think he liked me.

RUBY. Who?

HERBIE. She auditioned for Bing today.

A GIRL. Crosby?

LILY. *(Disdainfully.)* No. Rudolph.

(She exits.)

A GIRL. Bing Rudolph? Who's he?

(At this point, instead of **MONICA**'s *entrance, we hear* **JEANIE**'s *voice offstage.)*

JEANIE. *(Singing unaccompanied offstage.)*
OUT OF NOWHERE
CAME THE FEELING,
KNEW THE FEEL –

(Enter.)

Hi, kids!

ALL. Hi, Jeanie.

JEANIE. *(Exiting.)*
MARRIAGE TYPE LOVE.

LORAINE. I just saw them together!

ANOTHER. Larry and Jeanie?

LORAINE. They were in the chili joint on Eighth Avenue. As soon as they left the place they separated and walked on different sides of the street.

> *(A BOY at the left entrance signals to the other group and shushes them. LARRY is heard offstage, whistling [*"NO OTHER LOVE"*]. Everyone quiets down and looks innocent. He enters.)*

RUBY. Hiya, Larry.

LARRY. *(Awakening suddenly.)* Oh, hi Ruby... Hello, everybody.

> *(LARRY exits stage door.)*

HERBIE. It couldn't happen to two nicer people.

GIRL. Yeah! But what's going to happen when Bob finds out?

HERBIE. Gosh! I don't want to be around!

> *(Exit.)*

REMSON. How is she handling him.

A GIRL. She's telling him her mother's here from Chicago. That's why she can't see him.

BOY. She can't keep that up forever.

> *(Everyone exits.)*

(**BETTY** *enters.*)

RUBY. Hi, Betty.

BETTY. Hi, Ruby.

(**MAC** *enters.*)

Hi, Mac.

MAC. *(Very formally.)* How do you do, Miss Loraine.

(*He goes towards stage door.*)

BETTY. Hot for October.

MAC. Yeh. But good weather for the World's Series.

BETTY. *(Up cross to **MAC**.)* Yeh. What are you doing with yourself these days?

MAC. *(Cross downstage.)* Nothing much.

BETTY. *(Cross down left.)* Any truth about what I see in the columns – about you and Molly Burt being an item?

MAC. Could be.

BETTY. *(Cross to **MAC**.)* I used to know Molly quite well. We were in *Brigadoon* together.

MAC. That so?

(*Pause.*)

BETTY. Yeah! Boy! Is she a dull dish!

MAC. *(Cross below **BETTY**.)* Best I can do.

(*He crosses in front of her towards the stage door, **BETTY** swings him around.*)

BETTY. That's what you think.

(*He looks down at her. Their eyes meet for a long moment. Then he recovers.*)

MAC. You better go in and get dressed.

(She turns and starts off.)

(He calls her back.)

Betty...

(She turns towards back to him and comes toward him smiling.)

I've been meaning to speak to you about that seduction scene.

BETTY. What's wrong with it?

MAC. It's gone to hell, that's what.

BETTY. Charlie and I think that's our best spot.

MAC. I don't wonder. You sure look as if you enjoy it.

BETTY. *(Loving this.)* Charlie says the way we play it now is the way the author and director wanted it, and when you put me in the show you tamed it down.

MAC. That so?

BETTY. Uh huh! So, we've been heating it up a little each performance.

MAC. Well start cooling it off, y'hear? It's getting so obvious it's lost all its charm. It's just plain disgusting and vulgar!

BETTY. *(Delighted.)* Y'think so? Well, for instance... I mean where does it get bad? Shall we run through it, together and you can show me –

*(**BETTY** takes a **CARMEN** pose center and starts to clap her hands in rhythm. **MAC** looks pompous, reluctantly starts to clap his hands to the same rhythm. **BETTY** starts to dance and comes towards **MAC**. When she gets close to him **MAC** backs up looking embarrassed and he says:)*

MAC. Now wait a minute – wait a minute.

BETTY. Oh that's not the step, huh? Maybe you mean the Tango –

>   *(BETTY takes MAC and goes into another section of the dance, at the finish of this, BETTY is in a seductive pose and looking up at MAC.)*

Is that alright?

>   *(He nods.)*

>   *(They continue to dance until reach an even more seductive position.)*

MAC. *(Pushing her away.)* That's what I mean –

BETTY. Oh I see! What about this place?

>   *(She grabs MAC and they go into a whirling dance in the center of the stage. At the most embarrassing moment for MAC – BETTY speaks.)*

Is that too much –?

RUBY. *(Enters.)* What're you doing?

MAC. *(Flustered.)* Rehearsing.

RUBY. Who's rehearsing who?

MAC. I'm trying to fix that seduction scene. They're playing it like a burlesque show.

RUBY. I kinda like the way they do it.

MAC. *(To BETTY.)* You better go in and get dressed.

BETTY. Do you think we fixed it?

MAC. There's no fixing to do. You knew damn well what I want, Tame it down! That's what I want you to do. Tame it down!

BETTY. OK Mac. OK, I'll do my best, Mac.

> *(She turns and goes off, looking very happy.)*

MAC. *(To* RUBY.*)* Wanta slip across the street for a drink?

RUBY. I thought you never took a drink before a show.

MAC. I never do, but I just happen to feel like one.

RUBY. Look out, Mac. You start to break one rule, you may break another.

MAC. Nuts to you.

> *(He exits.)*

> (RUBY, *looking after* MAC, *smiles contemplatively.)*

> [MUSIC 20 – "THE BIG BLACK GIANT (REPRISE)"]

> (HERBIE *enters.)*

RUBY. Are theatre people crazier than other people?

HERBIE. Sure!

> *(Cross left.)*

RUBY. *(He starts to walk downstage as he ruminates.* I don't think so. They just <u>show</u> it more than other people. I think it comes from getting keyed up every night – getting scared and excited.

HERBIE. On account of that big black giant Larry's always talking about.

> *(He exits.)*

RUBY.
ONE NIGHT IT'S A LAUGHING GIANT,
ANOTHER NIGHT A WEEPING GIANT.

ONE NIGHT IT'S A COUGHING GIANT,
ANOTHER NIGHT A SLEEPING GIANT.
EV'RY NIGHT YOU FIGHT THE GIANT
AND MAYBE, IF YOU WIN,
YOU SEND HIM OUT A NICER GIANT
THAN HE WAS WHEN HE CAME IN,
BUT IF HE DOESN'T LIKE YOU, THEN ALL YOU CAN DO
IS TO PACK UP YOUR MAKE-UP AND GO.
FOR AN ACTOR IN A FLOP THERE ISN'T ANY CHOICE
BUT TO LOOK FOR ANOTHER SHOW.
THAT BIG BLACK GIANT
WHO LOOKS AND LISTENS
WITH THOUSANDS OF EYES AND EARS.
HE CLAPS HIS HANDS AND LUCK IS WITH YOU,
HE FROWNS AND IT DISAPPEARS.
HE'LL CHILL YOUR HEART
AND WARM YOUR HEART
FOR ALL YOUR LIVING YEARS.

> *(The spot fades out on **RUBY** and he exits. The traveller has been closed behind him and the next scene has been set.)*

Scene Seven: Betty's Dressing Room

(JEANIE, *pressing one of* BETTY's *costumes, looks up as she comes in singing gaily.*)

JEANIE. What are you so happy about.

BETTY. Mac says I'm overdoing the seduction scene with Charlie. He says it's obvious and vulgar – don't you get it? We're making headway, kid.

> (*She crosses and sits at dressing table and starts to undress. She takes her shoes off then puts her legs over chair and indicates to* JEANIE *to take her dungarees off.*)

> (JEANIE *comes down and pulls her pants off and hangs them on clothes rack.*)

> (BETTY *starting to make up.*)

Gosh, am I lucky, having you! ...When you asked me for the job I thought you were kidding. A college graduate, no less!

JEANIE. (*Smiling.*) I wanted the dough. My understudy pay stops this week. Summer's over. They don't need two understudies any more.

BETTY. You're a wonderful kid.

JEANIE. (*As she crosses toward ironing board.*) Wonderful, nothing. It's a break for me to be able to share this room with you – instead of dressing in that madhouse downstairs.

BETTY. (*Laughing.*) Whee! When those dames get together and start cackling together, that's something ...And it's always on the same subject.

JEANIE. (*Smiling.*) Yeh! Same thing you and I always cackle about.

BETTY. Yeh. I wonder why. I wonder why we let men take up so much of our lives. Why is it so important to me to make Mac jealous of Charlie? What am I after, anyway? To make him come up to me some night and ask me to go out with him? Would that be such a wonderful thing to happen? ...Yeh, it would.

(*She resumes powdering her face or whatever she is doing at this point in her make up.*)

I haven't heard much out of you lately about <u>your</u> love life. What's the matter with it?

JEANIE. (*With a nervous laugh.*) Oh, it's all right.

MAC'S VOICE. (*On microphone – in a loud speaker that apparently is in all the dressing rooms.*) Five minutes to overture! Five minutes to overture!

BETTY. OK Mr. Mac. I'll be ready. Stick around for the seduction scene tonight. I'm going to do a dance with Charlie that'll make you wish you were never born.

JEANIE. I fixed that zipper in your dress.

BETTY. Thanks. Boy, do I love to get into that dress. What a part! What a girl that Carmen! You know what I mean? All woman, and no complications. Just a bundle of uncomplicated passion.

JEANIE. Did it ever occur to you that Juliet might have more real passion than Carmen?

BETTY. No. Did it ever occur to you?

JEANIE. It's Larry's idea. You knew he's a wonderful director, Betty. All the understudies say the same thing. They say that he'll be one of the tops some day.

BETTY. Do you know how many times you've told me that?

JEANIE. (*Defensively.*) Told you what?

BETTY. *(Eyeing her closely.)* I bet you're going to miss those understudy rehearsals especially with such a sympathetic director. Ouch!

JEANIE. *(Putting a flower in* BETTY*'s hair.)* Hold your head still!

BETTY. You'll be getting stage-struck like me, maybe.

JEANIE. Could be.

BETTY. Boy, do I love to act.

[MUSIC 21 – "IT'S ME"]

(She rises and crosses up stage.)

All day long you can flop at everything you do. But at night – at night you know you're going to fool fifteen hundred people into thinking you're wonderful.

*(*BETTY *leaning back of dressing table chair – sings.)*

I'M COLORLESS AND SHY,
INHIBITED AND DULL.
MY ENTRANCE INTO ANY ROOM
IS FOLLOWED BY A LULL.
THIS DROOPINESS IN ME MIRACULOUSLY MELTS
WHEN I STEP ON A STAGE
AND MAKE BELIEVE I'M SOMEONE ELSE.
QUITE SUDDENLY
I'M MENTALLY AND PHYSIC'LY EQUIPPED
WITH MOST UNUSUAL QUALITIES –
IT SAYS SO IN THE SCRIPT!

JEANIE.
WHO IS THAT DELECTABLE DAME,
COOL AS CREAM AND HOTTER THAN FLAME?
WHO? WHO COULD IT BE?

BETTY.

IT'S ME! IT'S ME! IT'S ME!

JEANIE.

WHO'S THAT QUEENLY GIFT TO THE BOYS?

BETTY.

ALWAYS KEEN AND LOUSY WITH POISE?

JEANIE.

WHO? WHO COULD IT BE?

BETTY.

IT'S ME! IT'S ME! IT'S ME!
WHEN THE AUTHORS MAKE ME SAY
WORDS THAT MAKE ME WITTIER,
I FEEL JUST AS SMART AS THEY
AND, WHAT'S MORE, I'M PRETTIER!

JEANIE.

WHO'S THAT GIRL WHO'S GETTING THE WOWS?
WHO'S THAT BABE WHO'S TAKING THE BOWS?

BETTY.

IN A DAZE, I WONDER WHO IS SHE!
IMAGINE MY SURPRISE
WHEN ONCE I REALIZE
IT'S NOBODY ELSE BUT WONDERFUL, BEAUTIFUL ME!

MY PICTURE HANGS IN SARDI'S
FOR ALL THE WORLD TO SEE.
I SIT BENEATH MY PICTURE THERE
AND NO ONE LOOKS AT ME.
I SOMETIMES WEAR DARK GLASSES,
CONCEALING WHO I AM,
THEN ALL AT ONCE I TAKE THEM OFF –
AND NO ONE GIVES A DAMN!
BUT WHEN I START TO PLAY A PART,

    I PLAY THE PART OKAY.
    NO LONGER AM I NO ONE
    WHEN I'M SOMEONE IN A PLAY.

JEANIE.

    EV'RY MAN IS FLIPPING HIS LID
    OVER THAT PHENOMENAL KID
    WHO? WHO COULD IT BE?

BETTY.

    IT'S ME! IT'S ME! IT'S ME!

JEANIE.

    WHOSE HOT KISS FROM PASSIONATE LIPS
    PERPETRATES A TOTAL ECLIPSE?
    WHO? WHO COULD IT BE?

BETTY.

    IT'S ME! IT'S ME! IT'S ME!
    OH, WHAT I CAN PERPETRATE
    BY MY OSCULATION!
    JUST ONE LITTLE KISS, AND POUF!
    THERE GOES PERPETRATION!

JEANIE.

    WHO HAS LEARNED THE FORMULA WHICH
    SATISFIES THE SEVEN YEAR ITCH?
    WHO'S THAT DAZZLING PERSONALITEE?

JEANIE & BETTY.

    WELL, HERE'S THE BIG SURPRISE:
    HOT DOG! AND DAMN MY EYES!
    IT'S NOBODY ELSE BUT
    WONDERFUL, BEAUTIFUL ME!

    (During Coda music of song – **BETTY** *runs to dressing table, picks up fan and runs off as* **JEANIE** *bows her out of dressing room door.)*

[MUSIC 22 – "IT'S ME (INCIDENTAL)"]

(**JEANIE** *then gets her own dress off the hanger and puts a towel on her hair so that it won't be mussed as she puts her dress over her head. Then she hangs the towel up and starts to hook up her dress as* **LARRY** *enters. They embrace. He takes over the job of hooking her dress.*)

JEANIE. Remember what you said that first day? When two ordinary little people decide that they want to live with each other for the rest of their lives, they'll knock over anything that stands in their way.

LARRY. I remember.

(He holds her tighter.)

We've got to tell Bob, Jeanie.

JEANIE. I know. We've got to think of some good <u>way</u> to tell him.

(They embrace.)

I haven't found a good way to tell myself. I can't make myself believe that we did what we did today. Every once in a while I take the ring out of my bag and just look at it.

MAC'S VOICE. *(In loudspeaker.)* Everybody on stage. First Act! Everybody on!

LARRY. *(Whispering.)* See you later.

(They kiss again, he goes out quickly.)

[MUSIC 23 – "DRESSING ROOM"]

(JEANIE goes to her handbag, takes out ring and looks at it! She starts to sing:)

JEANIE. *(Singing.)*
IMAGINE MY SURPRISE

WHEN ONCE I REALIZE
IT'S NOBODY ELSE BUT
WONDERFUL, BEAUTIFUL –

MAC'S VOICE. Jeanie!

JEANIE. *(Suddenly realizing that she is late for her entrance on stage, she shouts.)* Me!

> *(She runs over to her dressing table, picks up the accessories to her costume and runs off.)*

Scene Eight: The Light Bridge

[MUSIC 24 – "IT'S ME (CHANGE OF SCENE)"]

(**BOB** and **SIDNEY**, *getting their lamps set for the finale of Act One.*)

SIDNEY. Well, I'll be glad to get down off this perch and stretch my legs.

BOB. You can't get down till they let you down. It's like being in jail.

SIDNEY. You know this first Act finale coming up is my favorite scene in the show? I'd like to go to a fancy night club like that some time – be out on the town.

BOB. With a girl like Carmen, huh?

SIDNEY. She'd be okay.

BOB. Tell me something, Sidney. Have you ever had another girl – I mean since you've been married?

SIDNEY. Sure. Plenty.

BOB. I bet you haven't had one.

SIDNEY. All right then.

(*Cross right.*)

I haven't had one. I don't see anything to be proud of anyway – cheating on your wife... Would you cheat if you got married?

BOB. Sure I would. That's why I don't get married... Right now I'm worse off than if I was married. I got a girl and I can't get to see her.

SIDNEY. (*Playing dumb.*) Yeh? Why not?

BOB. Her mother's in town. Got here from Chicago a month ago. She was only going to stay a week. But she's still here! Every week Jeanie says her mother is going next week... But she stays!

SIDNEY. *(Obviously knowing more than he is telling.)* That's a pretty tough deal.

Quick the effects!

> *(They both throw their lamps on.)*

BOB. *(After they have met their cue.)* So you wouldn't cheat. What about your wife? Are you sure about <u>her</u>?

SIDNEY. *(Suddenly very resentful at this suggestion.)* Aw, nuts to you.

> *(Getting worked up.)*

You just shut up about my wife!

BOB. Let's see. You live in Bayside.

SIDNEY. Y'better shut up! Leave my wife out of this or you'll be sorry!

BOB. What the hell will I be sorry about! ...Let's see, Bayside, that's about a half hour on the Long Island Railroad. That means you leave your house every night about seven. You can't get home before twelve – How do you know what she's doing all that time?

> *(SIDNEY is furious with BOB for talking like this about his wife. He can't hit BOB. He gropes for another way to get revenge.)*

SIDNEY. I know what she's doing all right... I know what somebody else is doing too.

BOB. *(Immediately sensing something from SIDNEY's tone.)* Yeh?

SIDNEY. And it ain't with her mother.

[MUSIC 25 – "INCIDENTAL ON LIGHT BRIDGE"]

(**BOB** *grabs* **SIDNEY**.)

BOB. You prove that or I'll tear you apart.

SIDNEY. If you feel like tearing somebody apart why not try it on the guy who's making a dope out of you?

BOB. Who?

SIDNEY. The Assistant Stage Manager.

BOB. Larry?

SIDNEY. Uh-huh.

BOB. Prove it.

SIDNEY. All right, I will. You come over and take my side of the bridge. I'll switch with you. And maybe if you look down there at his desk – at the right time – you'll see what I see every night... every single night.

BOB. What do you mean "the right time"?

SIDNEY. You know that part where Jeanie is carrying a lot of flowers on a tray?

(**BOB** *nods.*)

And Don Juan takes all the flowers and gives 'em to Carmen?

(*His voice shaking.*)

Then Jeanie goes off. That's when it happens. The same thing happens every night... Every night.

BOB. (*Huskily.*) Come on. We'll switch sides.

> (*Slowly* **BOB** *and* **SIDNEY** *move towards each other.* **BOB** *holds on to the rail to steady himself.* **SIDNEY**'s *face shows panic at the force he has set in motion and cannot stop. They switch sides. The music grows louder. The lights fade to black.*)

[MUSIC 26 – "FINALE ACT 1"]

(JULIET enter.)

JULIET.
>NO OTHER LOVE HAVE I
>ONLY MY LOVE FOR YOU
>ONLY THE LOVE WE KNEW
>NO OTHER LOVE HAVE I.

Scene Nine: A Nightclub

(The curtains part on a stage crowded with dancers, among whom are **BETTY** *as* **CARMEN** *and* **CHARLIE** *as* **ME.***)*

JULIET. *(Continued.)*
HURRY HOME, COME HOME TO ME
SET ME FREE,
FREE FROM DOUBT
AND FREE FROM LONGING

*(***CARMEN** *and* **DON JUAN***'s dialogue begins here, over* **JULIET***'s final chorus.)*
INTO YOUR ARMS I'LL FLY
LOCKED IN YOUR ARMS I'LL STAY,
WAITING TO HEAR YOU SAY:
NO OTHER LOVE HAVE I,
NO OTHER LOVE.

BETTY (CARMEN). Having fun?

*(***CHARLIE** *nods his head.)*

Then why don't you look happier?

*(***CHARLIE** *grins uncomfortably.)*

What have you got your mind on?

CHARLIE (ME). Nothing.

BETTY (CARMEN). Well, why don't you put it on me.

(The spot fades on **JULIET,** *as if she were fading from* **CHARLIE***'s guilty mind. He goes on dancing more happily with* **BETTY.***)*

(Now **JIM,** *as* **DON JUAN,** *comes on dancing with* **MISS OXFORD.***)*

CHARLIE (ME). You see that man that just came in. That's my boss.

BETTY (CARMEN). That so? Who's that with him?

CHARLIE (ME). Oh I don't know, some model or actress or somebody. He's always with a different one. They say he can get any girl he wants to get.

BETTY (CARMEN). That so? He couldn't get me.

CHARLIE (ME). How do you know?

BETTY (CARMEN). 'Cause <u>you</u> got me.

CHARLIE (ME). You're a doll, Carmen. Here I am, just an ordinary clerk who works in his office, and you'd rather have me than him – him with all those millions and yachts.

> (*They dance around for about four bars while* **CARMEN** *looks thoughtful.*)

BETTY (CARMEN). How many millions has he got?

CHARLIE (ME). Oh, I don't know, but it isn't less than fifty million.

> (**DON JUAN** *engineers his partner over in front of* **CARMEN** *and* **ME**.)

DON JUAN. Hello, my boy.

CHARLIE (ME). (*Nearly tongue-tied with, fright at being suddenly addressed by the boss who has never noticed him before.*) Hello, Mr. – Mr. –

JIM (DON JUAN). Meet Miss Oxford.

CHARLIE (ME). Please to meet you. This is Miss Carmen.

JIM (DON JUAN). How do you do?

> (*He takes* **CARMEN** *in his arms and dances off with her, motioning to* **ME** *to take* **MISS OXFORD**, *During the ensuing dialogue* **DON JUAN** *and*

CARMEN *and* ME *and* MISS OXFORD *continue to dance, as do the chorus, and meanwhile the stage moves over, revealing about ten feet of the off-stage scene.* LARRY *is at the Stage Manager's desk, which rides on as the stage moves over. About three quarters of the full stage remains and the dancing in "ME AND JULIET" can be seen while the dialogue is read.)*

You and I ought to make a good combination.

BETTY (CARMEN). Think so?

JIM (DON JUAN). Don't you?

BETTY (CARMEN). Maybe. Some day. I just don't like to start one course till I've finished with the other.

JIM (DON JUAN). Well, just remember the meat and potatoes are ready.

(Looking over at ME *dancing with* MISS OXFORD.*)*

As soon as you finish with the fish.

BETTY (CARMEN). I'll remember.

(Then the music starts going fast and they dance fast.)

(Now JEANIE, *wearing the costume of a nightclub flower girl, enters and walks among the dancers with a tray of flowers. Playing the scene* SIDNEY *has described to* BOB, *she goes up to* DON JUAN *and* CARMEN. DON JUAN *takes some orchids off her tray and gives them to* CARMEN. JEANIE *turns and moves toward the exit.* DON JUAN *delivers* CARMEN *back to* ME *and takes* MISS OXFORD. *The dance proceeds.)*

(Meanwhile **JEANIE** *exits, puts her tray of flowers on* **LARRY**'s *desk and then goes up to him as she apparently does every night, ready for her kiss. He takes her in his arms and kisses her.)*

(Suddenly a spotlight shines on them from the bridge. They both look up, panic in their eyes. They cling to each other like two terrified children and continue to stare up at the light as if fascinated and hypnotized by it.)

(The music becomes very loud at this point. The dancing on the stage becomes faster. **MAC** *enters, takes in the situation, and waves to* **BOB** *to take the lights off, but the light stays on.* **BETTY**, *onstage, looks up at the bridge, wondering why her spot has gone off. Then she looks into the wings and understands, and looks back at the bridge, frightened.)*

(Off-stage, **JEANIE** *pulls away from* **LARRY** *never taking her eyes from the bridge.* **MAC**, *in unheard dialogue, makes gestures to* **LARRY** *to beat it quick.* **RUBY** *comes on with a worried expression, as if already told about the crisis.* **MAC** *talks to him and* **RUBY**, *takes* **LARRY**'s *arm and leads him away.* **LARRY** *submits to this like a man in a daze.* **MAC** *then puts the tray in* **JEANIE**'s *hands and pushes her on to the stage. She walks across stage among the dancers, looking up frightened at the bridge. The lamp keeps following her as if* **BOB** *will not let her go. Terrified, she moves back toward the entrance on the right where* **MAC**, *in the wings, is waving wildly up to* **BOB** *to take the spot off her. As she reaches a certain point a* **GIRL** *looks up and screams. A sandbag comes down and knocks* **JEANIE**'s

tray out of her hands. **MAC** *pulls her off the stage, gets to his desk and shouts signals into his microphone, apparently ordering the curtain to come down while the dancers, terrified, go on with their routine, all keeping their eyes turned up towards the bridge. The curtain falls.)*

End Act I

ACT II

Scene One

[MUSIC 27 – "ENTR'ACTE"]

[MUSIC 27A – "ACT II OPENING CURTAIN"]

(Downstairs lounge of the theatre.)

(About one minute before the end of Act One of"ME AND JULIET".)

(On stage right is the lower part of a curved staircase leading to the auditorium upstairs. On stage left, well downstage, is the candy and lemonade counter at which **HERBIE** *presides. Up center is a door to the company manager's office The set is fairly shallow, so that it will seem crowded when the ensemble enter for their between-the-acts smoke.)*

*(***HERBIE*** is busy setting cartons of lemonade on top of the counter, taking them out of a very large box. Also on top of the counter are displayed some peppermint candies, life-savers, lozenges, and the usual assortment of lobby confections.* **TWO USHERS, SADIE** *and* **MILDRED** *come down the stairs. (On downstairs right).)*

MILDRED. Did you see the finale of the First Act?

SADIE. *(Cross left to counter.)* That was a funny one.

HERBIE. What was a funny one?

SADIE. *(Cross center.)* Just now in the finale one of the
spots came off a principal and followed a chorus girl all
around the stage!

MILDRED. *(Move down right.)* And then something
dropped from the top and nearly hit her.

HERBIE. *(Thoughtfully.)* That <u>is</u> funny.

MILDRED. This is a funny night all around.

> *(To* SADIE.*)*

Tell Herbie what happened to <u>you</u>, Sadie.

SADIE. *(Move to counter.)* Oh yeh. I was showing a guy and
his wife to their seats. They came in late. It was dark
on the aisle. His wife was walking in front of us and he
pinched me!

HERBIE. Where?

MILDRED. *(Points to her left buttock.)* Right there.

> *(On the hip.)*

SADIE. *(Pointing to the other side.)* No, here. I can feel it
yet – nearly.

HERBIE. What did you do?

SADIE. Before I could do anything the guy slips a five
dollar bill into my hand.

HERBIE. Then what'd you do?

SADIE. *(At counter.)* Gave him the two programs and beat
it up the aisle.

> *(Cross right.)*

HERBIE. Well, you got to hand it to a feller who pays as he goes.

*(Both **USHERS** up left off up left.)*

*(**RUBY** and **LARRY** come down the stairs, **RUBY** leads him straight over to the door, center, opens it with a key and pushes **LARRY** in.)*

RUBY. *(On stairs – move up center **LARRY**.)* Don't open the door if anybody knocks. Don't open the door unless I unlock it.

HERBIE. What's up?

RUBY. Bob caught Larry with Jeanie.

HERBIE. He'll kill him.

RUBY. He will if he finds him.

OFF-STAGE VOICE. Smoking in the outer lobby only.

HERBIE. Did he see you leaving the stage for the front of the house?

RUBY. That's what I'm afraid of. I think he did.

(He starts for stairs and turns back.)

If he comes down here, you don't know anything.

HERBIE. Check?

*(**RUBY** scampers up stairs as crowd comes on.)*

[MUSIC 28 – INTERMISSION]

LEMONADE!
FRESHLY MADE!
A BOTTLE OF ICE COLD COKE!

BORED PATRON.
I LOVE TO GO TO A THEATRE LOUNGE
TO ENJOY A NOISY SMOKE.

HERBIE.

LEMONADE!
FRESHLY MADE!

STARRY-EYED GIRL.

I SIMPLY ADORE THE SHOW.

BORED PATRON.

I WOULDN'T WAIT FOR THE SECOND ACT
IF I HAD SOME PLACE TO GO!

(Laugh.)

MUSIC LOVER.

I LIKE THE ONE THAT GOES:
DA-DI-DA-DUM,
DA-DI-DA-DUM,
DA-DI-DA-DUM.
MARRIAGE TYPE LOVE.

WIFE. *(To her husband.)*

I DON'T THINK IT'S RIGHT
TO BE SULKY ALL NIGHT
OVER ONE LITTLE BILL FROM SAKS!

BUSINESS MAN.

WHAT DO I CARE IF THEY BALANCE THE BUDGET,
AS LONG AS THEY CUT MY TAX?

(Laugh.)

MUSIC LOVER.

I LIKE THE ONE THAT GOES:
NO OTHER LOVE HAVE I.
HURRY BACK HOME TONIGHT!
IT'S ME, IT'S ME, IT'S ME –

HER COMPANION.

THAT DOESN'T SOUND QUITE RIGHT.

GIRL.

THE FELLOW BESIDE ME KEEPS DROPPING HIS PROGRAM
AND GROPING AROUND MY FEET.

BORED PATRON.

THE COUPLE BEHIND ME HAD GARLIC FOR DINNER
WOULD YOU LIKE TO TRADE YOUR SEAT?

GIRL.

I THINK THE PRODUCTION IS FINE,
THE MUSIC IS SIMPLY DIVINE
THE STORY IS LOVELY AND GAY –
BUT IT JUST ISN'T MY KIND OF PLAY.

HAPPY MOURNERS. *(All singing)*

THEY DON'T WRITE MUSIC ANY MORE
LIKE THE OLD VIENNA VALSES!
THE GUY TODAY WHO WRITES A SCORE
DOESN'T KNOW WHAT SCHMALTZ IS!
THE PLOTS ARE ALL TOO SERIOUS,
NO LONGER SWEET AND GAY.
THE AUTHORS WHO THINK
CERTAINLY STINK.
THE THEATRE IS FADING AWAY.

OH, THE THEATRE IS DYING,
THE THEATRE IS DYING,
THE THEATRE IS PRACTIC'LLY DEAD.
SOME ONE EV'RY DAY WRITES:
"WE HAVE NO MORE PLAYWRIGHTS,
THE THEATRE IS SICK IN THE HEAD."
SOME SINGER OF DIRGES
GETS EARNEST AND URGES
THE PUBLIC TO HAVE A GOOD CRY.

HERBIE.

BUT THE SHOW STILL GOES ON,
THE THEATRE'S NOT GONE.

HAPPY MOURNERS.
> WE WISH IT WOULD LIE DOWN AND DIE.
> WHY IN HELL WON'T IT LIE DOWN AND DIE?

STARRY-EYED GIRL.
> I THOUGHT THAT I'D LAUGH MYSELF SILLY
> ON THE EV'NING I SPENT WITH BEA LILLIE.

BUSINESS MAN.
> I SURE HAD TO HASSLE AND HUSSLE
> BUYING TICKETS FOR ROSALIND RUSSELL

SATISFIED PATRON.
> I JUST HAD A PICNIC AT "PICNIC"
> AND LOVED EV'RYONE IN THE CAST

HAPPY MOURNERS.
> YOUR TALK IS ABSURD!
> WHY, HAVEN'T YOU HEARD?
> THE THEATER'S A THING O' THE PAST,
> TRA-LA!
> THE THEATER'S A THING O' THE PAST.

STARRY-EYED GIRL.
> MY LOVE FOR MY HUSBAND GREW THINNER
> THE FIRST TIME I LOOKED AT YUL BRYNNER.
> AND BACK IN MY BED ON LONG ISLAND
> I KEPT DREAMING OF BRYNNER IN THAILAND.

BUSINESS MAN.
> I LOVE SHIRLEY BOOTH AND TOM EWELL.

ENTHUSIASTIC PATRON.
> THE "CRUCIBLE," BOY, WHAT A PLAY!

HAPPY MOURNERS.
> THE POOR LITTLE SCHMOS,
> NOT ONE OF THEM KNOWS

THE THEATRE IS PASSING AWAY –
HEY! HEY!
THE THEATRE IS PASSING AWAY!
THE THEATRE IS DYING,
THE THEATRE IS DYING,
THE THEATRE IS PRACTIC'LLY DEAD.
THE ONES WHO ARE BACKING IT
TAKE A SHELLACKING,
AND NEVER GET OUT OF THE RED.

ALL THE REST.
BUT ACTORS KEEP ACTING,
AND PLAYS KEEP ATTRACTING
AND SEATS ARE NOT EASY TO BUY.
AND YEAR AFTER YEAR
THERE IS SOMETHING TO CHEER –

HAPPY MOURNERS.
WE'D MUCH RATHER HAVE A GOOD CRY.

ALL THE REST. *(Spoken.)* Why the hell don't you lie down and die!

HAPPY MOURNERS. *(Sung.)*
THE THEATRE IS …

ALL THE REST.
LIVING!

HAPPY MOURNERS.
THE THEATRE IS …

ALL THE REST.
LIVING!

ALL.
WHY DON'T YOU LIE DOWN AND DIE!

OFFSTAGE VOICE. Curtain going up. Second Act. Curtain going up, etc.

SADIE. That's the one who pinched me!

MILDRED. To look at him you wouldn't think –

(*But as she says this the gentleman has passed by and done it to her. She squeals. The* **TWO USHERS** *exit as* **DARIO** *comes on and starts to gaze at several ladies, hoping that each one might be the one who is writing to him. As he gets near the counter,* **HERBIE** *addresses him.*)

HERBIE. Still looking for your gardenia woman?

DARIO. I am sick of this gardenia woman. Why does she hide from me? How long can a starving man live on flowers?

HERBIE. Must be some kind of a nut.

DARIO. Ah no, she is not a nut! You should see her letters. She is a poet! She has fallen in love with me, just watching me conduct. That's all she knows about me. Nothing more. Just how I look when I conduct the play. When I make beautiful music –

(**DARIO** *sips drink.*)

Ah no, she's not a nut.

HERBIE. She sounds like a nut.

(**HERBIE** *nudges him and points across to a lady who is wearing a gardenia.*)

(**DARIO** *leaves* **HERBIE** *and he and the lady gravitate toward each other as if drawn by some mystic impulse.*)

MRS. B. You're the orchestra leader, aren't you?

DARIO. Yes. Are you –

MRS. B. Let me have your cuff.

(*He holds his arm up.*)

(She takes a piece of lipstick and writes on it.)

This is my telephone number. When you go backstage will you give it to Charlie Clay, the one who plays Me?

DARIO. Charlie Clay!

(He exits.)

*(***JEANIE*** enters and goes to the office door.)*

HERBIE. He won't open it. Ruby told him not to. Ruby said –

BOB. *(Offstage.)* What's the difference who I am.

GEORGE. *(Offstage.)* Throw that guy out of here.

JEANIE. He's coming! Hide me!

HERBIE. Here!

(She gets behind the counter.)

*(***BOB*** enters.)*

BOB. Either one of them come down here?

HERBIE. Either one of who?

BOB. *(Going over to him.)* You know damn well who.

HERBIE. No I don't, Bob.

BOB. No I guess you don't – They're out here somewhere.

*(***BOB*** stops in front of the counter.)*

HERBIE. Gee, Bob, the curtains up, aren't you supposed to be –

BOB. Damn them! Damn them to hell!

*(He runs off as ***RUBY*** comes down the stairs, he stops short as he hears ***BOB*** offstage.)*

Anybody in there.

(Goes off left.)

*(**RUBY** points to box.)*

HERBIE. Jeanie! Quick!

*(**HERBIE** helps **JEANIE** into box, and puts lemonade cartons on top.)*

*(**BOB** comes back and **RUBY** stays on the stairs, unseen by him at first.)*

BOB. *(Muttering as he enters.)* That damned Mac – that lousy Stage Manager! He wouldn't move that ladder over so I could get down from the bridge. Gave them time to get away – damn him!

*(**BOB** stands frustrated, looking about him from one side to the other. Then he starts to move toward the counter.)*

HERBIE. *(Frightened.)* What do you want, Bob?

*(**BOB** slings **HERBIE** aside as he goes by him and takes a look behind the counter. There is, of course, nothing there. Then his eyes light on the box. He goes to the box and starts sweeping the empty lemonade cartons off the top. **RUBY,** in a last desperate attempt to save the situation, comes running downstage and shouts at **BOB.**)*

RUBY. Hey, Bob! What's the matter with you, you big drip?

BOB. *(Looking up quickly, unused to having anybody talk to him like this.)* What!

RUBY. *(Crossing to counter, and reaching over.)* Get back there on that bridge!

BOB. *(Straightening up.)* Who the hell are you talking to?

RUBY. I'm talking to you, you big gas bag ...

(**BOB** *takes a step toward* **RUBY**.)

(*Feeling his success,* **RUBY** *pours it on thicker
so that he can really divert* **BOB** *from what he
was going to do.*)

You got a job you're being paid for. You get the hell back
to that bridge or I'll call up the union. I'll tell them –

(**BOB** *reaches forward, pulls* **RUBY**'s *coat up
over his head, turns him around and lands
him seated on the floor.*)

BOB. Tell that to the union!

(*Cross to stairs – move down point to right.*)

You know one good thing about this lousy theatre? The
alley to the stage door and the front door are both on
the same street.

(*Cross to stairs.*)

A feller can stand at the bar across the way and nobody
can get out without him seeing it.

(*He goes over to stair.*)

RUBY. (*Rising.*) Keep an eye on him. Jeanie!

HERBIE. (*Crosses over to stairs.* **RUBY** *goes over to box
behind the counter and helps* **JEANIE** *out.*) He's gone.

(*A* **DRUNKEN GIRL** *enters from stairs.* **RUBY**
stands in front of **JEANIE** *trying to keep her
out of sight.*)

(*To* **DRUNKEN GIRL**.) Hey, lady, you're going the wrong
way, the second act has started.

DRUNKEN GIRL. (*Crossing to Ladies Room.*) I'll come
down here to the Ladies Room anytime I feel like it –
and I feel like it.

(She exits.)

[MUSIC 29 – "IT FEELS GOOD"]

*(**RUBY** leads **JEANIE** to the office door, unlocks it, **JEANIE** goes in. As **RUBY** locks the door behind her, the scene fades.)*

Scene Two: The Bar Across The Street

(**BOB** *is sitting at the end of the bar. A* **BARTENDER** *is pouring rye whiskey into a glass.* **BOB** *grabs the glass and swings it down. The* **BARTENDER** *starts to take the bottle away.*)

BOB. Leave it here.

BARTENDER. We're not supposed to –

BOB. Listen! I've been pushed around enough tonight, see?

(**BARTENDER** *puts the bottle back on the bar.*)

I'm not going to take any more... from anybody. Get it?

(**BOB** *starts to sing.*)
WHEN YOU LAY OFF YOUR LIQUOR YOU GET IN A RUT
AND FORGET THE FUN YOU HAVE MISSED FOR YEARS.

(*Pour drink.*)
THEN IT TOUCHES YOUR LIPS AND YOU GO OFF YOUR
   NUT,
LIKE A DAME WHO HASN'T BEEN KISSED FOR YEARS!

(*Drink.*)

(**BARTENDER** *goes off.*)
YOU FEEL THE WORLD GO DRIFTING BY,
AS IF YOU'RE ON A BOAT.
AND EV'RY TIME YOU DRINK SOME RYE
TO KEEP THE BOAT AFLOAT
A SMALL, BUT RED HOT BUTTERFLY,
FLUTTERS DOWN YOUR THROAT...

(*Rise.*)

IT FEELS GOOD,
NOT GOOD LIKE SOMETHING SWEET,
NOT GOOD LIKE SOMETHING BEAUTIFUL,
BUT GOOD LIKE SOMETHING STRONG.
IT FEELS RIGHT,
NOT RIGHT LIKE RIGHT OR LEFT,
BUT RIGHT LIKE IN AN ARGUMENT,
THE OTHER GUY IS WRONG!
IT FEELS GOOD TO FEEL HIGH,
HIGH ABOVE A WORLD OF WEASELS
AND THEIR *(Arm gesture.)* LOUSY WEASEL TALK.
A GOOD DRINK AND YOU FLY
OVER ALL THE THINGS THAT FRIGHTEN
ALL THE LITTLE JERKS WHO WALK.

YOU FEEL SMART,
NOT SMART LIKE SMARTY PANTS,
BUT SMART LIKE FINDING OUT THE TRUTH!
LIKE SOMEONE BANGS A GONG.
AND THAT GONG IS A SIGNAL
THAT THE ROAD'S ALL CLEAR,
WITH NO ONE AND NOTHING IN THE WORLD TO FEAR!
THE LIMIT FOR YOU IS THE SKY!
AND YOU ARE A HELL OF A GUY!

(Pound chest.)

AND IF <u>YOU</u> FEEL LIKE BREAKING UP A CERTAIN PLACE,
OR IF <u>YOU</u> FEEL LIKE PUSHING IN A CERTAIN FACE,
YOU ARE THE BOZO WHO CAN!
YOU ARE A HELL OF A MAN!
NOT A WEASEL,
NOT A LOUSE,
NOT A CHICKEN,
NOT A MOUSE,
BUT A MAN!

Scene Three: A sequence in Act Two of "ME AND JULIET"

[MUSIC 30 – "WE DESERVE EACH OTHER"]

(**JIM** *as* **DON JUAN** *enters right, as he dances centre* **BETTY** *as* **CARMEN** *enters left.*)

DON JUAN.

HIYA, CARMEN.

CARMEN.

HIYA, DON.

DON JUAN.

HOW YA FEELIN'?

CARMEN.

FIT!

DON JUAN.

FEEL LIKE DANCIN'?

CARMEN.

DON, YOU'RE ON.

DON JUAN.

BABY, THIS IS IT!

CARMEN.

LET'S CREATE SOME CHAOS.

DON JUAN.

THIS COULD BE THE NIGHT.

CARMEN.

LET US BE THE FIRST TWO WRONGS
THAT EVER MADE A RIGHT.
WE DESERVE EACH OTHER,
WE DESERVE EACH OTHER,
I'LL TELL THE WORLD THAT WE DO.

YOU AND YOUR MINIATURE SPARROW BRAIN,
I AND MY TINY I.Q.
WE DESERVE EACH OTHER,
LET ME TELL YOU, BROTHER,
I AM A DIFFICULT GIRL.
YOU'RE AN IMPOSSIBLE CHARACTER,
WHY DON'T WE GIVE IT A WHIRL?
I DON'T WANT TO REFORM YOU,
TO MAKE YOUR MISTAKES YOU ARE FREE.
BUT I JUST WANT TO BE CERTAIN
THAT YOUR GREATEST MISTAKE WILL BE ME!
IF YOU WANT TO WRESTLE,
I'M THE WEAKER VESSEL,
AND I'LL BE EASY TO SWERVE,
WE DESERVE EACH OTHER,
SO LET US TAKE WHAT WE DESERVE.

(As the curtain rises the dancing ensemble is discovered. They join **CARMEN**.*)*

*(***DON JUAN*** *in an elaborate dance.)*

Scene Four: Office of the company manager in the theatre.

[MUSIC 31 - "CHANGE OF SCENE"]

*(**LARRY** is pacing the stage. His coat is off. His fists are clenched as he walks. His face is tortured with worry and frustration. **JEANIE**, in her show costume, sits on the couch and watches him.)*

JEANIE. What are all those boxes over there on that safe?

LARRY. *(Stopping in his pacing as she hopes he would; he speaks in a dull, flat tone)* Those?... Mail orders. One pile has the letters and the checks in them, and the other pile is a record of the letters that have been answered.

(He resumes his nervous pacing.)

*(**JEANIE** continues to try to take his mind off what is troubling him.)*

JEANIE. I hear talk that the Stage Managers are going to ask you to put on their talent show this year. It would be good experience for you, wouldn't it? Betty says I'm getting stage struck – but she wants to be a great actress. I just want to be the wife of a great director.

LARRY. It takes a big man to be a director. You're married to a little man. A little man with no guts. That's why I'm in here hiding – hiding because I'm scared.

JEANIE. *(Trying to quiet him.)* Larry, you're just making yourself miserable. You –

LARRY. The first day I rehearsed you – I never told you because I was ashamed ...He grabbed me by the arms. I stood there, paralyzed with fright. He told me if I didn't keep away from you he'd kill me. I didn't answer him. I couldn't – couldn't talk. So damn scared of him I could hardly breathe!

> *(Towards the end of the speech, his voice has become shrill. He sits in chair by desk.)*

JEANIE. *(Smiling, studying him, her voice quiet.)* He said he'd kill you, and you married me anyway.

> *(Pause. She puts her hands on his shoulders.)*

I love you, Larry. I've loved you ever since that day we started to rehearse. I think you're a wonderful man, Larry – gentle, and understanding, and fun to be with. That's a lot of man for a girl to be married to. I couldn't expect to get a prize fighter thrown in with all that.

[MUSIC 32 - "I'M YOUR GIRL"]

ONCE AND FOR ALWAYS
LET ME MAKE IT CLEAR;
WHAT I AM TO YOU
AND WHAT YOU ARE TO ME.
I WANT TO TELL YOU
WHILE I HAVE YOU NEAR;
THIS IS HOW IT IS
AND HOW IT'S GOING TO BE.
I'M YOUR GIRL,
IT'S TIME YOU KNEW,
ALL I AM
BELONGS TO YOU.
ANY TIME YOU'RE OUT OF LUCK
I'M UNLUCKY TOO.
I'M YOUR PARTNER, YOUR LOVER, YOUR WIFE, YOUR
    FRIEND.
I'LL BE WALKING BESIDE YOU TILL JOURNEY'S END.
WITH YOUR ARMS AROUND ME,
I'LL BE YOURS ALONE.
I'M THE GIRL YOU OWN.

LARRY.
ANY TIME I'M OUT OF LUCK
YOU'RE UNLUCKY TOO.

JEANIE.
I'M YOUR PARTNER,

LARRY.
YOUR LOVER,

JEANIE.
YOUR WIFE,

LARRY.
YOUR FRIEND.
I'LL BE WALKING BESIDE YOU TILL JOURNEY'S END.

LARRY & JEANIE.
WITH YOUR ARMS AROUND ME
I'LL BE YOURS ALONE.
I'M THE ONE YOU OWN.

LARRY. Must be near the middle of the second act.

(He turns the loudspeaker on. It starts to play some music.)

JEANIE. Just about the middle.

(Now the lock in the door is turned. Their eyes shift to the door. The door is opened by **RUBY,** *and* **MAC** *comes through.)*

RUBY. You talk to them, Mac. I'll keep watch outside.

(He closes the door and locks it.)

MAC. Listen, kids. I don't want either one of you to go home tonight.

LARRY. Mac, I'll have to face this guy some time, Mac.

MAC. Maybe some time, but not tonight. He's out of control. He nearly broke up the show just now.

(*MAC switches off the lights.* LARRY *and* JEANIE *stands like statues. There is silence, then a knock on the window, with a heavy object.*)

(*A second's wait, then the window is broken.* BOB *puts his hand through, unlocks it, then pulls it open. The office being below the level of the alley, the window sill is even with the ground.* BOB *can therefore step through the window onto the sofa. He stands there for a moment silhouetted against the window. He has a wrench in his hand which he used to break the window. He slings it behind him so that it hits a radiator which can just be seen above the sofa, between the sofa and the window.*)

BOB. I thought I heard voices in here – I couldn't tell what they were sayin' –

(*Looking at* JEANIE.)

But I had a hunch that I knew one of the voices damn well.

(*He steps off the couch and turns to* LARRY.)

I told you what would happen, didn't I? I warned you!

(*He advances on* LARRY.)

(LARRY *backs up against the wall.*)

MAC. Just a minute there, Bob! You don't know what the hell you're doing.

(*He steps forward and grabs* BOB's *arm.* BOB *turns and plants one on* MAC's *jaw and* MAC *falls back on the floor. He's out cold.* BOB *goes back to* LARRY.)

BOB. I'm going to give you one chance. I'll let you go if you say to Jeanie what I tell you to say. Now listen close because it's your only chance. I want you to say: "Jeanie, I'm a lousy little coward and I don't love you enough to fight for you." Go on, say it!

(LARRY *stares at* BOB, *his face tense with the torture he is going through.* JEANIE *watches him. He turns toward her.*)

(BOB *senses that he's won. He gees to* JEANIE *and stands beside her.*)

Better be quick! It's your only chance. I'm not going to wait. Say it now! Say after me –

(*He puts his arm around* JEANIE *and pulls her close to him.*)

"Jeanie, I'm a lousy little –"

(BOB*'s touching* JEANIE *awakens* LARRY *and changes him suddenly from a sensitive, imaginative man to an instinctive animal. He springs on* BOB *like a wildcat.*)

LARRY. Take your hands off her!

(*Taking* BOB *by surprise with his agility and sudden strength he throws him to the floor and gets on top of him.* JEANIE *runs to the door and bangs on it.*)

JEANIE. Help, somebody! Help!

(BOB *grabs* LARRY*'s wrists and pulls his hands away, easily and slowly, showing how much stronger he is.*)

BOB. What the hell do you think you're doing?

(*He swings* LARRY *off his chest, still holding onto his wrists.*)

Want to fight, do you?

*(He throws **LARRY** on the couch.)*

*(**RUBY** enters and grabs **BOB**.)*

RUBY. Let him go, Bob! Get out of here!

*(**BOB** slings **RUBY** across the room. This gives **LARRY** a chance to get away, and he grabs **BOB** again around the neck, but this time **BOB** lifts **LARRY** right off his feet with his neck. The man who has the grip is the one who is being tossed around. They fall back against the pile of mail order boxes and the mail is scattered all over the floor. **MAC** comes to at about this time and rejoins the free-for-all. **JEANIE, MAC, RUBY** and **LARRY** all trying to tame **BOB** who like an angry bull slings them all away from him and keeps coming back at **LARRY**. **BETTY,** in her stage costume, comes running down the alley, peers through the window, sees what's up, jumps in and joins the fight. She is thrown against the wall near the safe. **MAC** lands near her. For a moment all are out of commission except **BOB** and **LARRY**. They grapple. **LARRY** is now fiercely defending his life. The two men veer toward the sofa, **BOB** on top of **LARRY**. They both lie still for a minute. Then **LARRY** starts to squirm slowly from underneath. **BOB**'s arms and legs are limp. He is apparently knocked out. **LARRY** gets up. Turns on light. **JEANIE** runs to him. **RUBY** is the first to go over and take a look at **BOB**.)*

His head hit the radiator.

BETTY. *(Out of breath.)* Is he dead, I hope?

RUBY. No. But he's out – good and out!

(**BOB**'s *five assailants are draped around the room, on chairs, on the desk, on the floor among the scattered mail-order envelopes – five breathless, panting, worn out people, their clothes disheveled, their hair mussed. They lie and sit and lean in silence for a few minutes.* **MAC** *is lying with head on* **BETTY**'s *shoulder, her arms around him. Slowly he looks up at her and realizes whose arm is around him. He leaps back as if he had been bitten by a rattler, jumps to his feet, goes over to the loudspeaker.*)

MAC. Next to last scene.

LARRY. Mac, we've a lot of cues coming up.

BETTY. Gosh, I've got to make a change.

JEANIE. Me too.

(*Both exit.*)

MAC. You go back and take over. I'll stay here with Ruby.

LARRY. But –

MAC. Go ahead.

LARRY. Sure.

(**LARRY** *exits.*)

(**RUBY** *closes the door.* **MAC** *fills a lily cup from the ice cooler, walks over and pours it on* **BOB**'s *head.* **BOB** *groans, half awakened.* **MAC** *turns* **BOB** *over. There is a bruise on his head where it hit the radiator.* **BOB** *sits up slowly,* **MAC** *and* **RUBY** *stand still, watching him.*)

(**RUBY** *goes to his desk, takes out a bottle of Bromo Seltzer, pours some into a lily cup.*)

BOB. Last thing I remember is having my hands on his throat.

> *(His eyes open wider. Fear crosses his face.)*

Did I kill him?

> *(**RUBY** and **MAC** look at each other quickly. Then **MAC** lowers his head as if he were silently assenting that **BOB** killed **LARRY**. **RUBY** follows suit. He looks down too. **BOB**, now completely awakened by sudden fear, turns to the window and starts to climb out, then ducks his head back quickly.)*

There's a cop at the head of the alley.

RUBY. *(Surprised and happy to hear it.)* There is?

MAC. *(Quickly.)* Of course there is. I phoned for a cop an hour ago.

BOB. All right. I'll take what's coming to me.

> *(**RUBY**, having filled the lily cup with water, passes the Bromo Selzter to **BOB**.)*

> *(**BOB** drinks it.)*

I couldn't help what I did. That little sneak stole my girl.

MAC. Girls don't get stolen, Bob. Watches get stolen. Money gets stolen. Girls don't get stolen. They go.

> *(**BOB** sits on the sofa thinking it over.)*

MAC. *(Quietly.)* Suppose I could get you off?

BOB. How do you mean, get me off? Who are you, the governor or somebody?

MAC. Suppose you had another chance. What would you do?

BOB. What the hell's the difference what I'd do?

MAC. You <u>have</u> got another chance, Bob.

> (**BOB** *looks from* **RUBY** *to* **MAC.**)

You didn't kill Larry.

BOB. *(Looking at* **RUBY.***)* Is that right?

RUBY. He knocked you out.

> (**BOB** *looks incredulous.*)

MAC. Well, he had a little help. The radiator back there.

BOB. *(Peeling his head.)* Where is he now? Did he go backstage?

> (*He starts for the door.*)

RUBY. They're <u>married</u>, you know.

> (*Both* **BOB** *and* **MAC** *turn quickly toward* **RUBY.***)*

MAC. Jeanie and Larry?

> (**RUBY** *nods.*)

BOB. How do you know? When?

RUBY. This morning down at City Hall they needed a witness. I was it.

BOB. *(Grimly, to himself.)* How do you like that?

> (*He goes over to the couch and sits down heavily.*)

RUBY. If you really mean that question, I like it fine. I think they'll do all right together.

BOB. *(As if he hadn't heard him.)* How do you like that?

MAC. He already told you.

> (**BOB** *looks at* **MAC**. **MAC** *looks him straight in the eye.* **BOB** *starts for the door.*)

MAC. Where are you going?

BOB. None of your damn business.

> (*He goes out.*)

RUBY. He may be going backstage.

MAC. I'll get there first!

> (*He climbs on the sofa and goes through the window.*)

> (**RUBY** *is about to leave through the door, when the phone rings.* **RUBY** *picks up the phone.*)

RUBY. Hello!

> (*Into the phone.*)

Oh, hello, Mr. Harrison... Really?

> (*His face lights up.*)

Maybe I can get him right now. He just left this minute. Just a minute.

> (*He runs to the window and calls out.*)

Hey, Mac! ...Mac!

> (*He peers down the alley and then goes back to the phone.*)

I was too late to get him, but I'll go right back and tell him. You're going to transfer him to the new show. Boy! Will he be tickled to death to hear this news!

> (*The set is now receding upstage and the lights are coming down.*)

Tonight? Why – er – everything was fine tonight. Yes, the show went very smoothly. Not a hitch, Mr. Harrison. Not a hitch.

(The lights fade as the set continues to move upstage.)

Scene Five: The Orchestra Pit

[MUSIC 33 – "FINALE ACT II (PART 1)"]

(As the lights go out on Scene Four, the show curtain comes down and **DARIO** *is spotted in the pit, conducting change music into the last scene of* "ME AND JULIET". *It is a different* **DARIO** *now. As he conducts he looks angrily around at the lady of the gardenia, if she happens to be there, and he holds his lapel out to call to her attention that he now wears a red carnation. He turns around and continues to conduct the change music, and the lights come up behind the curtain, which is a scrim.)*

Scene Six

*(Through the scrim the company is seen rushing into places, and the stagehands are just finishing setting the scene. **LARRY** stands in the center making sure that the scene is set before he gives the cue to ring up.)*

MAC. *(To **LARRY** in a loud whisper.)* Did Bob come back here?

LARRY. I haven't seen him.

*(**MAC** joins **BETTY** and **JEANIE**.)*

*(**LARRY** shouts to a carpenter.)*

Hey, Pete! Your third border is fouling that balcony piece!

(He goes upstage to supervise the adjustment.)

RUBY. *(Running on.)* Mac. I've got news for you! Mr. Harrison just called up. He's putting you in his new show!

MAC. Where's Betty? Baby, we're not in the same show anymore... you know what that means?

BETTY. No. Show me!

(She opens her arms.)

*(**MAC** moves in.)*

LARRY. Places everybody – places.

(He runs off right.)

*(**MAC** and **BETTY** are embracing ecstatically. The lights come up behind the curtain. The curtain starts to come up.)*

[MUSIC 33A – "FINALE ACT II (PART 2)"]

(**LARRY** *shouts from the wings.*)

Hey, Mac!

(**MAC** *is caught on stage as the curtain rises. Nimbly and ingeniously he dodges behind a boy and a girl, and knowing the dance routine well, does his best to keep masking himself until he is near the exit and is able to slink off the stage. At the end of the refrain the curtain comes down, but the lights immediately come up again behind the scrim, bringing us into the next scene.*)

CHORUS.
OUT OF NOWHERE
CAME THE FEELING
KNEW THE FEELING -
MARRIAGE TYPE LOVE.

WE WERE DANCING
AND YOUR EYELASH
BLINKED ON MY LASH -
MARRIAGE TYPE LOVE!

WE MADE A DATE,
COULDN'T WAIT FOR MY DAY OFF.

GIRLS.	**BOYS.**
NOW IT'S A THING	NOW! THING!
WITH A RING FOR THE	RING!
PAYOFF.	PAYOFF.
HM, PIGEON,	I'M YOUR PIGEON,
HM, ROAMING,	THROUGH WITH ROAMING,
HM, HOMING	I AM HOMING

CHORUS.
TO MARRIAGE TYPE LOVE,
MARRIAGE TYPE LOVE,
MARRIAGE TYPE LOVE AND YOU.

Scene Seven; Backstage

(The front of the "ME AND JULIET" curtain is seen only for an instant. Almost immediately the lights are thrown up behind the scrim revealing the company breaking up just as they do after a finale. The stagehands start to strike the set. The backdrop comes away.)

(LARRY enters quickly from the right crossing downstage left.)

LARRY. Stand by everybody! Don't take off your costumes.

GEORGE. *(Coming on from left.)* Keep your costumes on!

(Everyone stops wherever he is and listens.)

LARRY. I want to run the beginning of the first act finale. If we stay for five minutes now it will save us calling rehearsal tomorrow.

(Shouting across the stage.)

Lily, get over there and sing "No Other Love".

A GIRL. I saw Lily dashing out of the theatre as soon as the curtain hit the floor.

ANOTHER GIRL. She's singing over at Madison Square Garden.

LARRY. Oh yes. That benefit. I forgot... Jeanie! Stand in for Lily, will you dear?

(JEANIE runs over to extreme right.)

Take it from the second half!

(He indicates a vamp.)

Da da di dum-dum, AND!

[MUSIC 33B – "FINALE ACT II (PART 3)"]

JEANIE.
HURRY HOME, COME HOME TO ME,
SET ME FREE,

> (**BOB** *enters and crosses. Looks at* **JEANIE** *and crosses in front of her.*)

> (**JEANIE** *continues.*)

FREE FROM DOUBT
AND FREE,

> (**LARRY** *turns and sees* **BOB**.)

> (**JEANIE** *falters and finally stops singing as she sees* **LARRY** *and* **BOB** *facing each other.*)

LARRY. Bob, I've made a ten o'clock call for tomorrow morning for you and Sidney. All the lights on the bridge have to be re-angled. So you and Sidney be here at ten o'clock...

BOB. (*Hesitates for a moment, crosses over to* **LARRY** *as the* **COMPANY** *watch wondering what* **BOB** *is going to do.*) I didn't know you were married.

SIDNEY. Ten o'clock, okay Bob?

BOB. (*Crossing over left.*) I'll be here, I guess.

> (*He exits.*)

LARRY. (*To the* **COMPANY**.) Hold it, take it from the last eight.

> (*He brings his arms up to indicate upbeat.*)

And!

[MUSIC 33C – "FINALE ACT II (PART 4)"]

(**JEANIE** *sings at* **LARRY**, *who doesn't look her way, but watches his* **COMPANY**.)

LARRY. (*To* **COMPANY**.) Bend way back arms high.

JEANIE.	LARRY.
INTO YOUR ARMS I'LL FLY,	Now travel, travel all the
LOCKED IN YOUR ARMS I'LL STAY,	way around to your proper
WAITING TO HEAR YOU SAY	places.
NO OTHER LOVE HAVE I,	
NO OTHER LOVE.	Watch your spacing.

(*The curtain comes down slowly.*)

[MUSIC 34 – "EXIT MUSIC"]